P9-EDG-019

THE GLOBAL QUERY
"WE BRING YOU NEWS FROM THE EDGE!"

Featuring one of the best
investigative reporters in the business:
SAVANNAH "SAVVY" MCKINNON!

THE MONSTER OF MINNESOTA

When Savannah gets a phone tip about four mysterious deaths in northern Minnesota, her instincts tell her to follow up. Sure, maybe the people were killed by the lake monster known as Big Jelly. But Savvy thinks something—or someone—else did the dirty work . . .

"A fast-paced delight. A mystery with a blend of science and fiction that will leave readers looking for more *NEWS FROM THE EDGE.*"
—Laurell K. Hamilton, author of *Bloody Bones*

"This amusing SF novel mixes the investigative edge of *The X-Files* with a healthy dose of sleaze . . . Savvy's tabloid career offers plenty of potential."
—*Locus*

NEWS FROM THE EDGE
THE TRUTH EXACTLY THE WAY YOU WANT IT

Ace Books by Mark Sumner

NEWS FROM THE EDGE: THE MONSTER OF MINNESOTA
NEWS FROM THE EDGE: INSANITY, ILLINOIS

NEWS FROM THE EDGE

INSANITY, ILLINOIS

MARK SUMNER

ACE BOOKS, NEW YORK

If you purchased this book without a cover, you should be aware that this book is stolen property. It was reported as "unsold and destroyed" to the publisher, and neither the author nor the publisher has received any payment for this "stripped book."

This book is an Ace original edition.
And has never been previously published.

NEWS FROM THE EDGE: INSANITY, ILLINOIS

An Ace Book / published by arrangement with
the author

PRINTING HISTORY
Ace edition / February 1998

All rights reserved.
Copyright © 1998 by Mark C. Sumner.
Cover art by Jeff Walker.
This book may not be reproduced in whole or in part,
by mimeograph or any other means, without permission.
For information address: The Berkley Publishing Group,
a member of Penguin Putnam Inc.,
200 Madison Avenue, New York, NY 10016.

The Putnam Berkley World Wide Web site address is
http://www.berkley.com

Make sure to check out *PB Plug*,
the science fiction/fantasy newsletter, at
http://www.pbplug.com

ISBN: 0-441-00511-X

ACE®
Ace Books are published by The Berkley Publishing Group,
a member of Penguin Putnam Inc.,
200 Madison Avenue, New York, NY 10016.
ACE and the "A" design are trademarks
belonging to Charter Communications, Inc.

PRINTED IN THE UNITED STATES OF AMERICA

10 9 8 7 6 5 4 3 2 1

NEWS FROM THE EDGE

EDGE

INSANITY, ILLINOIS

ONE

THE IGUANA WORE GLITTER.

Terry Banyon thrust the unfortunate creature within inches of my face. "What do you think, Savvy?" he asked. "Does it look right?"

"Well . . ." I wrinkled my nose, but did not flinch away. Once you spent a few weeks around a tabloid as trashy as the *Global Query,* you were bound to encounter sights more disgusting than a badly decorated lizard. "That depends," I said carefully. "What's it supposed to look like?"

"A dinosaur," Terry replied. He pulled the lizard back a bit and surveyed it critically with his bright blue eyes. Terry was the sole in-house photographer at the *Query*. He was tall and broad-shouldered, with coalblack hair and these cute little dimples when he smiled—a source of much discussion among the other girls around the office. I had to agree, he was attractive. My only problem with Terry was that if you gave him half a brain, he would have half a brain.

"What kind of dinosaur?" I asked. It didn't really make that much difference to me. I was only hoping that if I stalled long enough, Terry would forget he had asked me to pass judgment on his talents as a lizard dresser.

"This Korean trawler picked up something in the South Pacific," Terry replied. "Mr. Genovese says it looked like an underwater dinosaur."

"Mr. Genovese says that, does he?"

I wondered if there really was any Korean trawler, or if it was just another of many ideas that had sprung full-grown from the mind of our editor in chief. Bill Genovese was not above inventing some news to fill a blank spot in the *Global Query*.

"So, does Irving look like a deep-sea dinosaur?" Terry asked again.

I tried to think of something polite to say. It was hard. As the resident model for all things reptilian, Irving had been featured in the *Query* dozens of times. His costumes were becoming more elaborate with each passing week. This time, in addition to the glitter, the poor iguana had been decked out with some custom rubber swim mitts over his feet and that perennial favorite, a cardboard sail on his back. It was enough to affront the dignity of any self-respecting lizard.

"I don't know," I replied at last. "Were there any deep sea dinosaurs? I thought dinosaurs were just a land thing."

"Sure there were," said Terry. "Like the Loch Ness Monster. Those long-necked kind with the little paddles."

Actually, plesiosaurs weren't dinosaurs. And even if they were, poor Irving bore no resemblance. Prehistoric reptile identification wasn't the kind of thing they taught you in journalism school, but at a paper where Nessie made almost as many headlines as Julia Roberts, it paid to know your Mosasaurs from your Megalosaurs. The only dinosaurs that looked anything like Irving were those that had played opposite Raquel Welch in movies where she wore a fur bikini.

I knew better than to tell any of this to Terry. "I guess he looks just fine," I lied.

Terry still didn't seem pleased. He heaved a heart-heavy sigh. "I'm so tired of making it up. If only Mr. Genovese would let me go on location, I could get pictures of the real monsters."

Of all the employees at the *Query,* I think Terry was the only one that really truly *believed* the stories we wrote. Whether it was Bigfoot stalking Seattle or the latest pineapple-walnut diet craze, Terry bought it all. Black helicopters carrying Russian troops over Idaho. Satan's picture on a peach pit. Egyptian pyramids on Mars. It all went into his empty head without encountering the least hint of resistance. Terry's only concern was how to get it on film.

I reached out and patted him on the arm. "You did great with Irving. And you're not really faking anything, you're just providing a sort of . . . visual aid for the story."

"A visual aid?" Terry repeated. He seemed puzzled for a moment, then he smiled suddenly and the Irresistible Dimples shone down at me with dizzying force. "That's good," he said. "Thanks, Savvy. I'll remember that." Lizard in hand, Terry turned and headed off for the *Query*'s tiny photo studio.

Reptilian crisis averted, I turned my attention back to the story currently glowing on my computer screen. There was an assignment rotation policy at the *Global Query*. Every couple of days, reporters were shifted from UFOs to celebrity dirt, from there to *dead*-celebrity dirt, then to general weirdness, and so on. Bill Genovese, our ever-thoughtful owner and editor, figured this would keep us all more flexible, so we could write any story that landed on our desk. Of course, it also kept anyone from learning very much about any one area. This was not a point that seemed to bother Mr. Genovese.

On the day of the sparkly iguana, the great wheel had delivered me that most dreaded slot: the miracle herb story. This one had real Pulitzer potential. GARLIC—CURE FOR AGING? I had all the ingredients of a complete multimedia presentation featuring: three whole pages of conjecture backed up by a doctor whose credentials wouldn't bear close scrutiny; a photo of a man who looked forty, claimed to be ninety, and was probably closer to thirty; and a big bundle of malodorous garlic cloves sitting in the middle of my desk.

The miracle herb was a headliner every third or fourth week in the *Query*. One issue it would be garlic, then it would be onions, or honey, or basil, or some god-awful combination of all four. The diseases followed a rotation of their own: baldness, weight problems, cancer, cholesterol, wrinkles, and aging in general. The blue-haired readership percentage of the

Query was way up there. Anything we could say about slowing down diseases of old age was guaranteed to move newspapers.

But I didn't care about the weeds or the conditions. I hated all the stories equally.

It wasn't the difficulty of the herb stories that made me dislike them—for the most part, you could just throw some dice, match a plant to a disease, and write the headline. What vexed me was more of a moral dilemma. Of all the assignments at the *Global Query,* the herb stories were the only ones that made me feel really slimy. Sure, the same issue might carry pieces on vampires, killer bees, UFOs, and sex changes of the stars. But none of those articles really did much damage to anything except our own tattered reputation. Downing a pitcherful of some noxious herbal brew might be enough to kill somebody.

I had been arguing that we should stop these stories for weeks. Mr. Genovese had countered with a chart of sales. A cure for baldness pulled in twice the suckers—that is, readers—as the latest gossip on President Clinton. A new arthritis treatment was right on top of the charts. When you handed Bill Genovese a moneymaker, he was not generally inclined to let fuzzy concepts like right and wrong get in his way.

I cast a furtive glance up the hall toward the editor's office, then looked down at my computer monitor and frowned. My article had been due on Genovese's desk yesterday afternoon and I still had nothing on the screen but a couple of limp paragraphs. It wasn't just that I had trouble writing the herb stories. This particular example of the breed was *particularly* idiotic.

The "expert" provided to back the story was a doctor somewhere on the high side of eighty. That might be a point in his favor, but if garlic did affect aging, it had done nothing for the doctor's own mental clarity. My three pages of notes were filled with the doctor's long rambling diatribes, including frequent references to Corregidor and the social policies of FDR. Worse, his rare mentions of garlic's stinky benefits had failed to produce even one phrase worth extracting. Mr. Genovese was not going to be pleased.

I mangled a few sentences in my third attempt at an opening paragraph, then gave up and grabbed the phone. If I couldn't get any work done, there were other, more pleasant chores.

My call was answered on the first ring. *"Green River Journal,"* said a familiar voice.

"Hi, Jimmy," I said, smiling stupidly at the receiver. "Are you playing receptionist today?"

There was a chuckle in response. "I thought I'd give it a try," said Jimmy Knoles. "After all, I've done everything else."

That was true enough. Jimmy had been working at one paper or another for longer than I had been alive. He had climbed the ladder from the copy desk at a small rural weekly all the way to the foreign desk at The *Washington Post*. He had filed reports from the deepest jungle and followed troops across the desert. Then, in a move I couldn't begin to understand, he had ditched his career to buy the *Green River Journal*. I guess everybody goes a little nuts sometimes.

"You too busy to talk?" I asked.

There was another soft laugh over the phone. "I'm supposed to go over to the Weight Patrol office in a few minutes. They're giving out awards to the people that lost over ten pounds last month. You know I can't miss a story like that."

I leaned back in my chair. "Well, with such world-shaking events, I won't keep you long. I just had a question about this weekend."

There was a long silence from the other end of the phone.

"Jimmy?"

"I'm here," he said.

"What's wrong?" I inquired. "I was only going to ask about the dinner on Saturday night. You know, so I can bring the right clothes."

Jimmy sighed. The easy laughter was gone out of his voice. "I'm starting to think this is a bad idea, Savvy. Maybe we should just skip it."

I felt a surge of feeling that was very near panic. Ever since I had come to town, I had been trying to build a relationship with Jimmy. At first it had been a purely professional interest. At forty-five, Jimmy had seen it all, done it all, and gotten tired of it all. He had made it to the *Post* while I was in grade school. He had already lived the kind of career that I wanted for myself. A few tips from a top-notch pro seemed like just the thing to lift me out of the *Query* and land me a *real* job.

But as I listened to his descriptions of adventures as a globe-trotting reporter and watched his gray eyes focus on scenes ten thousand miles away, I realized that I was interested in a lot more than Jimmy's career advice. We had worked up the scale from a business relationship, to friendly lunches, to that uncomfortable state that was a little more than friendship and a little less than romance. And that was as far as it had gone.

This weekend looked like my big chance to tip the scales away from the "just good friends" column. Jimmy had been asked to speak at the annual Midwest Journalists Association meeting. I was thinking about going when to my surprise, Jimmy had actually asked me to go *with* him—as in two people, one car for six hours. Two hotel rooms, unfortunately, but Jimmy's invitation seemed to imply that the actual use of that second room might be in doubt. This could turn out to be a lot more than a business affair.

Apparently Jimmy was beginning to regret that moment of weakness. "Savvy?" he said. "Are you still there?"

"I'm here. Jimmy, we've been planning this for weeks," I said, trying to keep my voice calm. "You can't back out now."

There was another pause from his end of the line. "Jimmy?"

"I'm here," he replied in his smooth coulda-been-an-announcer voice. "I'm just concerned that we're moving a little too fast. We should be careful not to rush into anything before we're ready."

It was my turn to sigh. "I've known you for almost a year. This is the slowest 'rushing' in history."

"When you get as old as me, you slow down."

"Stop that." I pressed my lips together and got myself under control. I was about to come up with the perfect reply when I heard the thud of heavy footsteps approaching. "Can we talk about this over lunch?" I said quickly.

"I don't—"

"Thanks!" I said. "See you in an hour or two."

I dropped the phone back in its cradle and just managed to get my hands poised above the computer keyboard when Mr. Genovese came stomping down the aisle between the cubicles, waving a sheaf of papers. "Ms. McKinnon!" he shouted.

I jumped and whacked a few random keys on the computer. "It's almost done," I lied.

Mr. Genovese's wide face was cut by a heavy frown, but the expression provided no clue to his mood. Bill Genovese would frown if he won the lottery. "What's almost done?" he asked.

I gave myself a firm mental kick and did my best to look innocent. "Nothing. What's up?"

The editor glared at me for a few more seconds. "It's the cold-call line. We've been getting a lot of volume."

I repressed a shudder. The cold-call line was another of Mr. Genovese's wonderful inventions. We published a toll-free number in each issue of the *Query* so that people could call in to report their own strange stories. The line was manned twenty-four hours a day. If there was anything worse than writing miracle herb stories, it was spending hours listening to the whining of the nutcases on the cold-call line.

"I had the midnight shift last night," I said. "In fact, I didn't get off until a couple of hours ago. You aren't going to make me take more calls, are you?"

"That's not the problem," said Genovese. He searched

through the papers in his hands, produced a dog-eared form, and slapped it down on my desk. "Did you take this call?"

I looked down at the page. There was no mistaking my own distinctive scribbles. "Sure."

The paper held the first contact report on a call that had come in near the end of the shift. The caller, a woman named Myrtle, stated that the appliances in her house had come to life and were menacing her. The vacuum cleaner had chased her down the hall. The oven had snapped at her. Everything mechanical was in on the act. A side-by-side, frost-free, avocado-green refrigerator had gone so far as to eat Ms. Myrtle's favorite Pekingese pooch. Apparently, since she was able to make the call, the telephone had remained loyal during this appliance revolution.

"I thought this was pretty good," I said. "Might make decent filler."

Without replying, Mr. Genovese dropped a second form over the first. "And this one?"

The second form concerned a call that had also come sometime in the early-morning hours. According to the man on the phone, fissures in the earth were spitting thick smoke into the sky above his apple orchard. A "Volcano Erupting in the Heartland?" story might have been good, but then the caller had added that little men in pin-striped suits were also emerging from the fissures. The farmer suspected they were IRS agents. Somehow, that seemed like too much of a good thing—even for the *Query*.

"Yeah," I agreed. "That report's one of mine."

Mr. Genovese nodded. "That's what I thought." He

dropped the rest of the stack on my desk, a stack that contained at least a dozen calls.

"I didn't do all these!" I protested. "I only got six calls all night."

"These came in early this morning," said the editor.

"Then why give them all to me?"

Mr. Genovese folded his arms across his chest. "You're the one with the fancy journalism degree. Why don't you do a little investigative journalism and see if you can figure it out?" With that, he turned and stomped back down the aisle.

I stared gloomily at the papers. Most of them had been filled in by Porter Henshaw, second only to Terry Banyon in the *Query*'s hierarchy of the gullible. Porter's small, prissy handwriting described each call in painful detail. One report described a flight of UFOs hanging over a barn—nothing too odd there. But the next page, which featured a whole flock of snow geese emerging from a toilet, was genuinely weird. One man's television was delivering dark prophecies from God. A woman named Tilly delivered a lengthy tale that included walls that dripped Silly Putty and giant rabbits wearing sunglasses. Compared with the reports that followed, the giant-rabbit lady was tame.

I went through all the reports once, flipped the stack over, and started again. The whole bunch came from people that were way over the edge, but that was true of ninety percent of what came in over the cold line. I didn't see anything that connected this batch.

After reading them a third time, I started to pick them up and tell Mr. Genovese I was stumped. Then I spotted it. What the events had in common was not in the incident reports themselves. It was at the top of every page.

I gathered the sheets and hurried to Mr. Genovese's office. "They're all from the same town," I said as I came through the door. "Or at least from the same area. Not everyone provided an address, but all the phone numbers start with the same digits."

Mr. Genovese looked at me from the padded leather chair behind his disgustingly clean desk. I harbored a momentary thought that he might congratulate me on my sleuthing, but he soon ended that thought. "Took you long enough to spot it."

I ignored the jab to my ego. I hadn't always been perfectly tactful in expressing my disdain for the *Query*'s journalistic standards. Mr. Genovese was not about to miss an opportunity to let me know that I was still just a snot-nosed college-girl reporter, and he was still the editor in chief, founder, and principal owner.

"What do you think?" I asked. "Could it be some kind of hoax?"

"That's what I figured," said Mr. Genovese. "It wouldn't be the first time some joker got the idea of flooding the lines." He rubbed his hand across the dark stubble that persistently covered his wide chin. He appeared at the office every morning clean-shaven, but by lunchtime, the stubble would be heavy enough to give his face a Fred Flintstone shadow. "But there's something that makes me think there's more to it than a few kids that got tired of asking about Prince Albert in a can."

I studied the scribbled forms for a few moments, trying to see what else I might have missed. This time

I was stumped. "Two of the calls came from the same number," I said. "The rest of them are all different. Of course, people can give any number they want. What makes you think they're not all fake numbers?"

"I did a little something called follow-up, Ms. McKinnon. You ought to try it sometime." Mr. Genovese tapped the black telephone at the corner of his desk. "I called all the numbers on these sheets."

I gave him a few moments to finish, but it was clear that he expected further prompting. "And?"

"And there's no answer," said Mr. Genovese. "No answer at any of a dozen phone numbers. Wouldn't you think that's odd?"

"They could all be at work."

"They could be, but I doubt it. I checked the phone company. All those numbers are in Meridian, Illinois. Four of them are business numbers. One of them is the damn chamber of commerce."

I thought about that for a moment. No answer at the chamber of commerce did seem more than a little odd. "Okay," I said. "So something is going on. What are we going to do about it?"

"You," said Mr. Genovese. "You're going to do something about it."

"Me?"

He nodded. "Meridian is less than a hundred miles from here. You've been wanting to get out there and do some on-the-spot reporting. Well, here's your chance. I want you to go up to Meridian and see why this little town has become psycho central."

I pressed my lips together and tried to remember the number-one rule for getting along at a newspaper:

Thou Shalt Not Yell at Thy Editor. "When you offered to let me do more field reporting, I thought it would be more like checking out the latest Loch Ness investigation, not driving a couple of hours across wheat fields."

Mr. Genovese nodded slowly. "All right. If you've changed your mind about doing fieldwork—"

"I didn't say that! I just thought it would be something better." When there were a thousand wackos all lined up to tell us their story over the phone, field assignments were rare as hen's teeth at the *Global Query*. Only the fact that I nursed my first extracurricular activity into a front-page story gave me another shot at leaving my desk behind.

Mr. Genovese snorted. "You want a vacation in Scotland, you take it on your own time. You want to get out of here, you take the assignments you're given. Who knows? You do a good job with this one, maybe the next one will be better."

I was about to give in when this big red warning sign appeared at the front of my mind: YOU HAVE A DATE WITH JIMMY.

"I don't suppose it can wait till Monday?" I asked.

"This is the news, Ms. McKinnon. It doesn't wait until you find it convenient."

A dull ache began to throb behind my eyes and I had to clear my throat before I could squeeze out my next words. "Then maybe you should assign someone else."

I wouldn't have thought it possible, but Mr. Genovese's frown grew even deeper. "What's this? After all the talk you've given about getting better assignments, I'd think you'd jump at a chance to prove yourself."

"I would. It's just that I've got plans for this weekend."

"Plans?" Mr. Genovese made a rumbling sound, like thunder that was getting rapidly closer. "Listen to this, Ms. McKinnon. You earned a lot of credit around this office with the work you did up in Minnesota. This is your chance to build on that work. Don't throw it away on some *date*." The way he said "date," you would have thought it was some kind of hideous curse.

If Jimmy had been even the slightest bit more enthusiastic on the phone, I might still have said no. "All right," I said as I stood up. "I'll go."

"Good," said Mr. Genovese. "And take Mr. Banyon with you."

"Terry?" The idea of driving around for hours with someone that actually believed in UFOs, Atlantis, and surviving dinosaurs did not thrill me. "Why do you want me to take Terry along?"

"You're a fine writer, Ms. McKinnon, but you are a rotten photographer. If we had better pictures on the Minnesota story, our sales would have been ten times higher."

He had a point. "All right," I said. "I'll go collect Terry."

"Cheer up, Ms. McKinnon. Should this story really turn out to be nothing but juvenile delinquents exercising the toll-free system, you may yet be back in time for your date."

Somehow, I didn't think that was likely. I turned and headed for the door.

I was almost out of the office when Mr. Genovese called me back. "Ms. McKinnon. These plans of yours . . ."

"Yes?"

"They wouldn't have anything to do with our mutual acquaintance James Knoles, would they?"

"Why do you ask?"

"No reason," said Mr. Genovese. He was rubbing his stubbled chin with his hand again, and his mouth was partly hidden. If I hadn't known better, I would have sworn he was smiling.

TWO

THERE ARE SOME PEOPLE WHO TEMPT FATE ALL THEIR LIVES AND get away with it. I know why—fate is too busy picking on me to notice anyone else.

It had been cloudy all morning. For September in St. Louis, that usually meant we were in for long soggy drizzle. But not this time. Ominous black thunderheads were boiling up over the hills to the west, and the rest of the sky was tinged a bilious green that promised torrents and tornadoes. Despite the threatening appearance, the skies had not given up a drop of rain all day. I was foolish enough to think it would wait another ten minutes.

I charged out of the office as soon as lunchtime arrived, determined to get to the *Journal* before Jimmy had a chance to dodge me. But obviously spotting me on the sidewalk sans umbrella was more temptation than any storm could bear. Six blocks out from the *Global Query,* and still five away from Jimmy, an arc of blue-white lightning sizzled across the sky. That was the signal for water to begin falling in drops the size of ping-pong balls.

My hair was flattened in a second, and my one absolutely genuine, dry-clean only, wool cardigan dress was plastered against me almost as fast.

I ran on through sheets of rain that blew over my face with such force that I could have used a set of gills. By the time I made it to the door of the *Journal,* water was gurgling ankle-deep along the sidewalk and a miniature Niagara was splashing down my back. I flung open the glass door and stumbled into the lobby.

Compared with the chaos at the *Query,* the offices of the *Green River Journal* were quiet as a tomb. The battered metal receptionist's desk was unattended. That was none too surprising since, as far as I knew, there had been no receptionist for years. The only one there to greet me as I dripped onto the well-worn carpets was an exceptionally large bass mounted on the paneled wall behind the desk.

"You'd be right at home outside," I muttered to the fish. Shivering, I clutched my wet arms and walked across the lobby. The air-conditioned office was cold enough on a normal day; soaking wet, it was enough to raise a bumper crop of goose bumps on every inch of exposed skin.

I stopped in front of a mirror at the end of the hall and studied my reflection. What I saw was not encouraging. My hair was a total loss. It hung around my face in thick damp masses, like the moss that dangles from trees above alligator-infested bayous. The wool dress had been snug to begin with— purchased in the wake of my eternal optimism over losing weight in the near future. Now it was embarrassingly tight, not to mention wet. By the time it dried, I was figuring it would make a decent dishrag.

For a moment I considered retreating. I could slip back into the storm and never let Jimmy see me looking like a drowned rat. But Mr. Genovese wanted me on my way to cover the crank-phone-call story within the hour. If I was going to see Jimmy before he left for the convention, it was now or never. I ran my fingers through my rain-soaked hair, tugged the shrinking dress over me as best I could, and tried to pretend I didn't look as bad as my reflection.

A pair of old news-wire machines guarded the hallway leading to the newsroom, chattering away inside glass cases. In the age of the Internet, the machines themselves were probably worth more as antiques than as practical tools, but Jimmy kept the wire machine running nonetheless. Snatching the news off the folded sheets of printout fit Jimmy's romantic notions of how a paper should operate.

As I walked past, one of the machines sounded a bell. It rang once, then twice. I stopped for a second, but there was no third ring. I walked on. Two bells marked a fairly important story, not the assassination of the president, but certainly more than a new hairstyle on the first lady. Whatever it was, it wasn't likely to be anything I could use at the *Query* — unless the Associated Press was leading off with a story about Bigfoot.

Shaver Wilcox sat at a drafting table in the center of the newsroom, trimming thin strips of newsprint. Shaver was a black man of undetermined, but un-

doubtedly immense age. His hair, his eyes, and even
his skin were all working toward the nameless color of
dust and old peanut shells. Age had not brought him
any obvious wisdom. I had been working as a volunteer at the *Journal* for more than six months, and in all
that time he had never said anything that could
remotely be considered nice. He was a spiteful old
man, with a sharp tongue, a fondness for vile cigars,
and absolutely no redeeming features—except that he
was practically the only man left on Earth who knew
the workings of the *Journal*'s ancient presses.

As I came dripping into the room Shaver's gaze
drifted up from the newsprint. He lifted one of his
evil-smelling cigars from the table, clamped it between his lips, and shook his head slowly. "You know,
it's sad."

I gritted my teeth. "What's sad?"

"You'd think by now you would have learned to put
down the lid *before* you sat down." Shaver chuckled
dryly to himself, each laugh producing a cloud of
noxious fumes. I've been told that he has mellowed
considerably over the years—which was a frightening
thought.

I slogged my way to the other end of the newsroom
without receiving any further abuse and knocked on
the door of Jimmy's office. Without waiting for an
answer, I pushed open the door and stepped inside.

Jimmy Knoles looked up at me. "Is it raining
outside?"

"No," I replied. "I took a quick dash through the car
wash on my way over."

"Very efficient," Jimmy said with a nod. He pulled

open the top drawer of his desk, closed it, opened the next drawer, and pulled out a small white towel. "Here," he said, tossing it across to me. See if this helps."

I took the towel and dabbed at my face and arms. It was not enough to really dry me, but it was a help. "You always keep a towel in your desk?"

Jimmy shrugged. "It's a golf towel. You never can tell when you're going to need to polish a club."

I took a closer look at the towel I'd been vigorously rubbing against my face and spotted faint but identifiable grass stains. "How lovely."

"You should go through the car wash more often," said Jimmy. "It suits you."

I tugged at my shrinking dress. "Thanks . . . I guess."

Jimmy laced his fingers together and put his hands behind his head. "So what do you hear from Wild Bill? Are you going to be around this weekend?"

"No," I replied. "He wants me to follow up this story in Meridian."

"Oh," said Jimmy. That was all, just "oh."

I put my damp hands on his desk and leaned toward him. I pretended not to notice the water dripping onto his work. "The least you can do is look a little disappointed."

Jimmy frowned for a moment. "I'm heartbroken," he said, but even as he said it a smile crept back onto his face.

"Jimmy!"

He held up his hands. "Look, Savvy. I'm sorry you

won't be there for the conference, but I'm not sorry we're going to miss the rest of it."

"But we had this thing planned out for weeks!" Even to myself I sounded like I was whining.

"Look, Savannah—"

I held up a hand and stopped him right there. "Whenever somebody starts using my whole name, it always means trouble. This sounds like the start of one of those Gee-I-think-you're-a-nice-girl speeches I used to get back in high school right before I was dumped for some cheerleader."

Jimmy looked surprised. "Why would anyone do that? You really are a lovely girl, Savvy."

Okay, give the man ten points.

"In fact, I can't imagine anyone at your school was more attractive."

Make it twenty.

Jimmy reached across the desktop and covered both of my hands with one of his. "I think you're smart, sexy, and you've got the makings of a hell of a journalist."

Cash in your chips, ladies and gentlemen. We have a winner.

"But . . ."

I groaned. "Why is it when anyone says something nice about me, there always seems to be a 'but' attached? If you think I'm so great, then why won't you go out with me?"

"Because you're also only twenty-five," Jimmy continued. "You're not only young enough to be my daughter, my real daughter is older than you."

"So what?" I replied. "Age doesn't mean anything."

It was my set speech, but I wasn't sure that even I believed it. Age did matter to most people. It had mattered to me—right up until the day I met Jimmy.

Jimmy ran his fingers through his graying hair. "We don't have anything in common. You grew up in a totally different world."

The conversation was going downhill fast. "I'm not some brainless bimbo," I reminded him. "I know my recent history. I'll bet you that I know more about Watergate or Vietnam than anyone else in this office."

Jimmy raised an eyebrow. "Including me?"

"Maybe. Try me."

He shook his head. "Some other time. You may be right, but I'm not talking about the evening news. I'm talking about all the little things." He gave a very heavy sigh. "You make me feel like Steely Dan singing 'Hey, Nineteen.'"

"Who's Steely Dan?" I asked, opening my eyes as wide as I could.

Jimmy looked like his heart had stopped. "You don't know Steely Dan?"

It was my turn to sigh. "Of course I do. But I don't think you'd be happy if I named every member of The Who and gave you a bio of Jimi Hendrix." I pulled my hands free of his and backed away from the table. "You're just looking for an excuse."

That didn't get an answer. Jimmy looked across the newsroom as if he desperately wished I was not there.

"Is that it, then?" I asked. "You don't want to go out with me?"

"No," Jimmy replied quickly. "I mean, yes, I do want to go out with you. I just want to make sure that

I want to go out with you because you're you, and not because your're twenty-five." He stopped and gave me a weak smile. "Does that make sense?"

I nodded and stood up. "Sure. You think I'm nothing but Lolita with a steno pad."

"God no, I didn't say that." He looked terribly embarrassed. I don't think I had ever seen James Knoles, hardened international journalist, looking embarrassed before. I rather enjoyed it.

For half a second I thought about letting him off the hook. I could say that all was forgiven and promise to see him next week. Jimmy would go back to being the gruff but lovable editor, and I would be his part-time Lois Lane. But I only gave it half a second. After months of going after Jimmy, it was time I either hooked him or put up my equipment.

"Go to your conference alone," I said.

"Maybe we could—"

"No," I said, cutting him off. "I want you to go alone. You go to this conference and think about us. When you come back, we'll talk." I stood up straight and tried to look dignified despite the water running down my legs. "In the meantime I've got a story to cover."

To my disappointment, this pronouncement drew nothing but a thoughtful nod from Jimmy. "Maybe you're right," he said. "A weekend apart might be just what we need."

Now I didn't have to pretend to be mad. "Fine," I said. I turned and started for the door.

"Bring back a good story," Jimmy called after me. "And be careful out in the field."

I rolled my eyes. "I know you think I'm young, but I'm not seven, okay? Besides, I'm only going right across the river."

"Just don't let your guard down," said Jimmy in his best Sage Journalist tone. "Whenever you go out in the field alone, there's danger."

I pulled on my coat. "It's Meridian, Illinois, not Medellín. Besides, I'm not going alone. Terry's going with me."

Jimmy's brows pulled together. "Who?"

"Terry Anderson. You know—tall, black hair. He's the *Query*'s one and only photographer."

Jimmy frowned. "He's that kid that used to play football, right?"

There was much more concern in Jimmy's voice when he asked about Terry than when he thought I was heading off on my own—a very interesting development. I put on my best poker face and shrugged. "I think he did play football in college, but Terry's not a kid. He's the same age as me."

"And he's going with you out of town."

"Yeah."

Jimmy pressed his lips together for a moment, then nodded. "Well, you're not going far. I'm sure you won't be gone overnight."

"I don't know," I replied. "Like you say, anything can happen once you're out in the field." I gave him a quick smile. "Have fun at your little convention."

"It's a symposium," Jimmy replied.

I waved a hand in casual dismissal. "Whatever." I opened the door to the hallway, turned, and gave him what I hoped was a dazzling smile. "I'm sure Terry and I will be fine."

Before Jimmy could think of a reply, I shut the door and hurried down the hall. I wasn't sure if I should be happy or sad—it was a confusing scene. I only hoped it wasn't the last one Jimmy and I ever played together.

THREE

"BIGFEET HAVE RETURNABLE TOES."

I took my eyes off the highway for a moment and stared over at Terry. "What did you say?"

"Returnable toes," Terry repeated. "Bigfeet have returnable toes."

"That's what I thought you said." I turned back to the road and watched my wipers valiantly trying to part a Red Sea's worth of rain as we rolled slowly along the clogged interstate.

Miles in St. Louis have an odd sort of elastic property. If you happen to be east or west of your target, there is a wealth of highways waiting to speed you along. But should you have the misfortune of desiring a trip north or south, you've got little choice but to squeeze onto I-270 with what always seems like half the population of the county.

I had gone by my apartment and changed into a driftwood-colored turtleneck, brown cords, and matching low-heeled pumps. It was appropriate field-reporter

gear, conservative and wonderfully dry. Then it was back
to the office to get Terry. Now, over an hour later, we
were only halfway to Meridian.

During that hour Terry had favored me with his
theories on everything from how Atlantis had been
destroyed by the Ark of the Covenant to how dinosaurs remained hidden in underground homes beneath
the panhandle of Texas. It was one thing to know that
Terry was a sucker for all the weird and wondrous
stories that were printed in the *Query*. It was quite a
different thing to have to live with that belief in a small
confined space for hours at a time. The most frightening part was that some of the nonsense he was
spewing had been drawn straight from stories that I
had written.

Terry thumped a finger against the book he held in
his left hand. "See, this guy says all the bigfeet tracks
out west have five toes."

"Yeah, so?"

"So, all the ones around here have three toes."

"I've heard that." I wasn't sure what Terry was
thinking, but at least I could see where he was coming
from. For as long as people had been tracking furry,
manlike critters prowling the woods of North America,
the footprints of those west of the Rockies had been
oversized versions of human feet. Those in the East
were another matter. Eastern Bigfoot displayed a more
varied pattern. Some specimens had four toes, some
three, and some had only two. Cryptozoologists suggested these pedal peculiarities meant there were more
than one species of upright apes in our forests. I had

always suspected it meant that hoaxers in the East had more imagination than their Western counterparts.

Terry's explanation was more original. "It's like cats," he continued.

I tried my best to ignore this statement, but after a few seconds my curiosity overwhelmed my good sense. "Cats have returnable toes?"

"No," said Terry. "Just their claws."

It finally dawned on me what he was trying to say. I glanced back over at him. "Do you mean *retractable*?"

Terry nodded enthusiastically. "That's it. Cats have retractable claws, so maybe Bigfeet have toes like that."

I stared at him for a moment, trying to tell if he was making a joke, but his bright blue eyes were frightfully serious. "Sure," I said. "I'll bet you're right. And they probably can change colors, you know, like a chameleon. That would explain how they can disappear so easily."

Terry might believe in every creature found in the pages of the *Query,* but he was apparently a total stranger to the beast called sarcasm. He smiled at my suggestion of a color-changing Bigfoot. "That's a good idea, Savvy." For a moment he was silent, then he rubbed one hand across his chin. "I wonder if that's how those pterodactyls in the South hide."

I gritted my teeth. We hadn't even made it out of the city and my temptation to throttle Terry was already reaching irresistible levels. "Maybe," I said. "But I think we should concentrate on what's going on in Meridian right now, don't you?"

Terry leaned forward and peered through the windshield as if he could see all the way to Illinois. "You think there's something like Bigfoot in Meridian? Or maybe aliens?"

I shrugged. "It's hard to say. We'll find out when we get there. You need to stay objective. Collect all the information before you make a judgment."

To my great relief, Terry fell into silent contemplation of the adventure ahead. A few minutes later traffic began to break up. I swerved around a rusty van and splashed along the left lane for another dozen miles. As the bridge into Illinois appeared around a turn, I fought my way across the traffic and swooped down the ramp onto a state highway.

"I thought Meridian was in Illinois," said Terry.

"It is," I replied with a nod. I pulled over to the side of the road and consulted the directions Mr. Genovese had scribbled down for me. "We're going to Illinois, but Meridian is on an island. The only way to get there is by using a ferry."

Terry opened his mouth in surprise. "A what?"

"A ferry. You know, a boat for cars?"

"Oh," he said sadly. "One of those."

I glanced over at his disappointed face. I opened my mouth and started to say something, then closed it quickly. Better that I didn't even *know* what he thought I had meant.

I got the car back onto the road and drove along slowly until I saw a small sign on the right reading SILVER BELLE FERRY. At that point I almost turned back. The road leading to the ferry was dirt, or rather, mud. In the driving rain, it appeared to be nothing but a series of puddles connected by patches of muck. I fully expected to sink up to my hood as soon as I turned off the highway. Only a vision of Mr. Genovese kept me going—I could just imagine what he would say if I came back and said I couldn't get the story because I was afraid of muddying up my car.

My fears of the road were not quite justified, but they were close. We bumped, splashed, squished, and floundered our way through the mud for almost a mile. I wrestled the gearshift from first to second, then back down to first as the conditions disintegrated. Twice the nose of the car dipped into potholes so deep, the brown water sprayed across the windshield and the engine came close to stalling, but at least one of the four cylinders hung in there and we sputtered and stumbled our way to the edge of the river.

Terry pointed through the rain streaked windshield. "Is that the ferry?" he asked.

I desperately wanted to say no, but I nodded instead. "I guess it is."

Despite the aggrandized name, the *Silver Belle* looked more like the poster boat for rust. As far as I could tell, the whole thing was nothing but a dented and time-corroded barge equipped with a smoking diesel engine at one end and a cabin the size of an outhouse at the other. Beneath and beyond the shabby boat, the Mississippi stretched out into the distance. The silt-stained water foamed and churned under the assault of the storm.

"This is going to be cool," said Terry.

"Oh, yeah," I said. "Really cool."

The door on the tiny cabin swung open and a man

in gray coveralls emerged. He stood there in the pouring rain for a moment, gnawing on a half-eaten apple. Then he walked slowly across the flat deck. When he reached the stern of the ferry, he pulled a metal bolt from the side railing. At once a gate at the back of the boat flopped down to splash in the mud, forming a steep ramp. The man raised his hand and waved to us.

I looked at the ferryman and shook my head. "He can't be serious. I wouldn't want to ride that tub in good weather. Surely he's not going to try and cross now."

"I don't know, Savvy," Terry replied. "He looks like he really wants us to come on the boat."

In this observation, Terry was—for once—correct. The man in the coveralls stood at the top of the ramp, making slow circles with his hand as he waved us forward. Lightning lanced into the river behind him, casting stark black shadows along the muddy bank.

Reluctantly, I put the car in gear and rolled toward the back of the rusty tub. My fear of this crumbling ferry was high, but it didn't quite match my fear of Bill Genovese—yet.

The fender scraped the ramp on the way up, and the ferry bobbed alarmingly, but eventually we were on board. The small deck had been optimistically marked into six spaces. The man in the coveralls walked in front of me, waving toward a corner slot in the front row. I ignored him. Since I was the only one stupid enough to dare the marshy road and this death trap of a boat, I figured I deserved any place I wanted. I took a position dead in the center, as far from the water as I could get.

As soon as I turned off the engine, the storm seemed to double in strength. Rain mixed with hail racketed off the hood of the car and bounced from the deck of the ferry. It hissed into the river around us like a basket of snakes, stirring up a foam that gave the whole Mississippi the look of a giant cappuccino—not that I would want to drink it.

The wind picked up and the ferry bobbed like a cork on the waves. My stomach lurched as the boat skewed around to the right. River water washed over the bow and retreated in streamers of brown.

"Wow," said Terry. "This is going to be fun."

I stared at him. With that one statement he had firmly cemented my opinion of his mental abilities. "Fun?"

There was a tap at my window. I turned to see the man in the coveralls looking down at me. Up close, he was even less impressive than his vessel. He was an older man, somewhere in the range of fifty-five and sixty-five, with thin gray hair plastered to a spotted scalp and a patina of grime that not even the storm could wash away. His brown eyes were the same color as the silt-choked river. I cranked the window down a crack, admitting a stream of rain that splashed against my car seat. Despite the water sluicing down his hooked nose and the beads of hail bouncing from his forehead, the man opened his mouth in a yellow-toothed grin.

"Afternoon," he shouted over the noise of waves and rain. "I'm Cap'n Finley." He pronounced his title exactly as it was spelled on the boxes of sugary cereal.

"Is the ferry running?" I asked, hoping for a negative reply.

"Oh, sure," he said with a nod. "See, it takes more than a little dampness to put me out of business. Where is it you wanting to go?"

"We need to get over to Meridian."

"Meridian?" The ferryman scratched at his growth of beard. "You're a day late for going over there."

"A day late? Don't you go over to Meridian every day?"

"Sure," replied Cap'n Finley. "But, see, you already missed the festival."

"What festival?"

"Apple Festival." The man looked toward the north bank and wiped the rainwater away from this face. "That's the big deal over there, see."

"Well, we're not going for the festival," I said. "We just need to get to the island. Will you take us?"

The ferryman nodded. "I expect I could," he said. He turned toward me and stood silently for a few moments, then he stretched his neck and looked over the roof of my car. "I could take you, but expect we better wait till a few more customers show."

I looked over my shoulder at the empty stretch of mud road. "How many customers have you had today?"

"None."

"Then how long do think we might have to wait?"

The cap'n shrugged. "See now, that's what's hard to say. Could be a few minutes. Could be some hours."

"Don't you think you could just take us on over?"

He considered it for a moment. "Well, see, I could take you by yourselves, all alone like. But every time as I run with just one car, it costs me money."

Suddenly, the cap'n's meaning became clear. "And how much money would that be?" I asked.

He rubbed his chin again. "I usually get five for the trip, see, but that's when I'm loaded up. For me to run empty, I expect that would run about twenty bucks extra."

I smiled at him. Obviously this man had never heard of an expense account. "No problem," I said. "We'll pay."

The ferryman's yellow-toothed grin returned. "All right, then. Let's get going." He took an enormous bite from the apple and shoved the half-eaten fruit into the pocket of his sodden coveralls. Then he turned and walked off toward the stern. Lightning flared again as the old man pumped madly on the winch to raise the ramp. No sooner had it clanged against the stern than he hustled up to the tiny cabin and jerked open the door.

Just as the ferryman was about to step inside, he suddenly paused, threw out his arms, and turned his face up to the storm. A convulsive shiver shook him from head to toe.

Gooseflesh sprouted on my arms. I had forgotten to roll up the window, but this time the bumps on my skin had nothing to do with cold or rain. Something was very wrong.

Cap'n Finley stepped into the cabin and shut the door. A moment later the diesel engine rumbled to life.

"Here we go," said Terry. He sounded like a kid looking forward to a trip on the roller coaster.

"Yeah," I said. "Whoopee." I rolled up the window and locked the door.

The ferry's engine gave a cough and a belch of black smoke drifted through the rain. As the diesel revved up, the deck shook so hard that my car began to vibrate. With a groan of stressed metal, the ferry eased away from the bank.

Almost at once we began to slip downstream. The bow of the ferry turned sharply left and the boat shuddered as it moved against currents and waves. Already I was wishing for some Dramamine. Near the bank, the water was merely choppy, but as the ferry moved toward the heart of the channel, the swells rose into mounds of water that would have done any ocean proud. We rose suddenly on the crest of a wave, then fell into a trough with a splash that sent walls of water rushing from the side of the square ferry. Waves pounded against the boat like hammers beating on a drum. As we sailed up and down the back of another swell, the car bumped on the deck, bounced, and skidded a few inches to the right.

"Wow!" shouted Terry. "That was something."

I nodded. My heart was far too high in my throat to squeeze any words past. I was in the middle of the river, in the middle of a raging storm, something was wrong with the ferry pilot, and there was an idiot in my car. Scratch that—two idiots. No matter how intimidated I was by Mr. Genovese, or how much I wanted to impress Jimmy, I should never have been stupid enough to get into such a situation. It was one thing for a reporter to risk her life to bring back information on some critical story. But no story that had ever appeared in the *Global Query* was worth this.

We crested another huge wave, and the car slid a few more inches to the right. I looked out the window, gauging the distance between the wheels and the edge of the ferry. By my calculation, we had at least a dozen bumps left before we would be driving on the bottom of the river. I hoped there were no more than eleven waves ahead.

To my great relief, we passed through the roughest part of the stream and moved into water that, while far from calm, was at least less than furious. Through the rear window of the car, I watched the Missouri bank turn into a distant shadowy form behind the torrents of rain. The Illinois shore was still invisible through the fog and storm, but at least I was starting to feel a sense of progress.

For long minutes both banks were invisible. Then the island of Meridian appeared ahead. As we closed in I saw a steep, hilly bank and a handful of houses high on the slopes. The rhythm of the ride changed as the chugging engine slowed. The crash of the waves against the sides of the ferry faded to a gurgling. Even the slashing rain began to slacken as the storm finally eased.

I breathed a sigh of relief. "Looks like it's smoothing out."

Terry nodded. "Yeah, that's too bad." He pointed toward the rain-soaked shore. "But I thought we were going over to that place."

"We are," I replied with a nod.

"Then why are we turning?"

"Turning?"

I looked up to see that the bow of the boat was swinging quickly away from the shore and pointing downstream. My fear came back double strength. The engine had not just slowed, it had stopped completely, and the ferry was drifting powerless before the river. The shoreline was sliding past at an ever-more-rapid pace.

"Where do you think we're going now?" asked Terry.

"New Orleans," I replied.

FOUR

"YOU KNOW," SAID TERRY, "THERE ARE CATFISH AS BIG AS school buses in this river."

"Shut up," I replied. I shoved open my door and stepped out onto the swaying deck.

Terry looked at me with astonishment. "Savvy, I don't think we're supposed—" I slammed the door, cutting off the rest of his warning.

Dampness appeared to be my destiny. The rain had slowed, but it was still heavy enough to soak my hair and dress as I edged carefully toward the cabin at the front of the ferry. The black metal of the deck was covered with enough accumulated grease that the rain beaded up and ran off in rainbow-colored streams. It was pretty—in a sort of grungy industrial way—but it made for slippery footing.

Terry pushed open the passenger door and leaned out. "What are you doing, Savvy?"

"Nothing," I shouted. "Get back in the car and shut the door."

Terry nodded and obeyed.

I trudged through the rain to the small cabin. Close up it looked so much like a portable toilet that I suspected the little booth had been redirected to its current status after doing time along a parade route or at some construction site. The hard plastic door was closed tight, but the rain left me in no mood to respect anyone's privacy.

"Mr. Finley?" I called, and pounded against the plastic. There was no answer. "Captain, are you okay?" Still nothing.

I grabbed the handle and pulled. The door swung open with a creak, revealing a small steering wheel, a window that had been roughly cut through the front of the cabin, and our charming captain. The old ferryman turned his face slowly around to look at me. "You still here?" he mumbled.

A blush of embarrassment heated my cheeks and I stepped back from the door. The man was naked. From the top of his balding head, down past his pale knobby knees, he wore not a stitch of clothing. The grimy coveralls were wadded in a heap at his feet, along with some unidentifiable undergarment whose color might most generously be called gray. For a moment I wondered if he might have been using the tiny room for its original purpose.

I spun away from the door and looked at the bank sliding past. "What are you doing in there?"

Apparently the question was a difficult one. Cap'n Finley grunted a few times and cleared his throat, but he produced no answer that I could understand.

"Are we still going to Meridian?" I asked.

"Meridian?" The man gave a sharp, choking laugh. "We can't go to Meridian."

There was a grinding crunch as the boat bounced across a sandbar. I staggered away and tottered for a moment at the edge of the deck before a fortuitous wave sent me careening back toward the cabin. "You said you would take me to Meridian!" I shouted at the naked man.

"I did?" he said. He reached up and scratched at his spotted scalp.

"Of course you did," I said. "I promised to pay you twenty-five dollars for the trip."

The man shook his head. "Twenty-five would be okay," he said, "but we can't go to Meridian."

"Why not?"

"Because," said Cap'n Finley, "to get to Meridian you got to have a boat."

"Are you nuts?" I demanded. Which was, I'll admit, an awfully stupid question to ask a man who was standing naked in a porta potti floating in the middle of a river. "We're *on* a boat!"

The man responded with a howl of laughter that sent literal shivers running along my spine. "We're not on a boat!" he declared.

"We're . . . not . . . on a boat," I repeated carefully. I took a step back from the cabin. "Then where are we?"

"'S'obvious," said the ferryman, slurring his words together. He stepped out of the cabin and started toward me across the deck. "We're on a —"

Wherever the man thought we were, I never got to hear it. Two steps away from the cabin, his right foot found a patch of muddy grease, and before he could finish his sentence, his bald head was moving down and his bare posterior was moving up. His skull cracked against the metal deck with a noise like a well-delivered bowling ball and his white arms flew out to the side.

I dropped down beside him, my knees grinding painfully against the filthy metal deck. "Finley!" I shouted. "Captain? Are you all right?" Rain splashed into the man's unshaven face, but he didn't show any sign of waking up. I swallowed hard and put a finger against the ferryman's neck to check his pulse.

The passenger door on my car popped open. "What happened?" called Terry.

"The ferry driver fell down!" I shouted back. I was relieved to feel a steady thumping against my fingertips. At least the man wasn't dead.

Terry climbed out the car and hurried around to my side. His eyes went wide as he looked down at the unconscious captain. "Did he fall out of his clothes, too?" he asked.

"No, he didn't fall out of his clothes. He was . . ." I shook my head. "Never mind. Help me get him up."

I put my arm under Finley's bare shoulders, but before I could lift him the ferry struck some new obstacle with enough force to spin it completely around in the water. I went to my hands and knees on the deck and barely avoided falling full-length across the naked ferryman.

Cap'n Finley opened his eyes and looked up into my face. An entirely different kind of smile came over his disreputable-looking features. "Hi, darlin'," he said. From a few inches away his breath was a fog of bourbon. "You come here often?"

I got up fast. "Are you going to steer this boat?"

"Boat?" The man shook his head. "I already told you this ain't no boat." He closed his eyes again and rolled over on his side.

Terry paced around the dock. "What's wrong with him?"

I pushed wet hair away from my face and shrugged. "I think he may be drunk."

Terry frowned. "He didn't seem drunk back when he picked us up."

"No," I agreed, "but who knows how much he drank on the way across the river."

"Should we get a doctor?"

"Probably. But before we can get a doctor, we're going to have to get off this boat."

I turned around slowly. The rain was slacking off and the sky was getting lighter. Thirty yards away, trees leaned out over the boiling river, but there was no sign of a dock and only a little way ahead I could see the downstream end of the island approaching.

"How are we going to get off?" asked Terry.

"Stay here and watch this guy," I instructed. "Make sure he doesn't wake up and walk into the river."

Terry nodded. "Okay," he said. "What are you going to do?"

I shrugged. "I'm going to steer the boat." I marched over to the plastic cabin and looked inside. The controls of the vessel were refreshingly simple—if more than a little crude. The steering wheel looked as if it had been lifted from a Dodge Dart, and the only other control was a dangling cord attached to a heavy spring.

Through the roughly cut window at the front of the little room I could see nothing but the brown spread of the river. I took a deep breath, grabbed the wheel, and gave it a turn. The ferry shuddered and there was a groan of stressed metal. Slowly the bow swung around and the shore came into view through the window, but it did little to change the direction of our travel. The ferry was now traveling backward down the river.

I reached for the cord overhead and gave it a tug. At once the diesel engine roared and our progress down the river began to slow. In a few seconds the ferry came to a halt relative to the shore, then began to work its way against the flow of the water. The upstream progress was considerably slower than the rapid pace we had taken down the river, but at least we were moving in what I hoped was the right direction.

Terry put his head through the cabin door. "The ferry guy's still sleeping," he said.

"That's good, but you better watch him."

"He's snoring," said Terry. "I don't think he's

getting up soon." He shook his head sadly. "It's terrible."

"What's terrible?" I asked.

Terry shrugged. "What drinking does to people. That's why I never drink. Drinking makes you stupid."

I couldn't help but smile at the thought. If drinking diminished Terry's IQ, it might force him into negative numbers. "That's a really good idea."

After a few minutes of struggling upstream, a patch of gray concrete came into view on the shore. It wasn't much of a dock, but at this point it looked wonderful. I turned the bow of the ferry toward the sloping gray rectangle, gave the throttle cord a jerk, and managed a landing that was about as smooth as the average line in a single's bar.

I unwrapped my white-knuckled fingers from the steering wheel. "Okay, now let's see if we can get the ramp down so we can get off the boat."

"What about the ferry guy?" asked Terry. "What are we going to do with him?"

I stepped past Terry and looked down at the fallen Cap'n Finley. There was a strong temptation to leave the old drunk where he lay, but he had taken a serious fall. "I guess he goes with us," I said reluctantly.

I worked on getting the ramp down and left Terry to wrestle the cap'n into his discarded coveralls. I might be stuck with transporting the man, but I wasn't about to let him lie naked on my backseat. By the time I had the ramp down, my hands were covered in grease and sliced by frayed cables. Just as I was finishing up, the ferry groaned and skidded a few feet along the concrete. I turned around to see Terry still struggling with Finley's clothing.

"We need to get off of this thing before we end up back in the river," I called to him.

"I'm kind of having a problem," Terry replied without looking up.

"What's wrong?"

"His zipper's kind of stuck on, well, on . . ." Terry's voice trailed off.

"On what?"

"On his, well . . ."

"Never mind." I moved around beside Terry and took hold of Finley's ankles. "Let's just get him in the car—on his back, please."

The ferry scooted another foot as I started the car. The damp engine was reluctant to start, but with a little cursing and grinding the car rolled across the small deck and down the ramp. As soon as the rear wheels left the boat, the ferry rose a few inches in the water. That was all it took for the current to pry the boat away and send it tumbling downstream.

Terry stared out the back window with his mouth gaping open. "The ferry guy's going to be mad at us when he wakes up."

"He's got no reason to be mad at anyone but himself," I replied, watching the boat slip out of sight. "Come on. We need to call someone and warn them before that ferry runs into a casino boat."

The road on the island was at least two notches ahead of the trail we had followed to get to the ferry.

It was drier, and patches of it were actually paved. There were no houses near the ferry, but within a few miles I spotted a small bungalow perched on a hilltop. The house was painted an unlikely shade of purplish pink—somewhere between mauve and a bad bruise—but the yard looked well tended. More important, there were phone and electric lines running up to the building. Anxious to shed our extra passenger, I pulled into the driveway.

Terry climbed out of the car with me. I was surprised to see that he had a camera in hand.

"Why are you bringing that?"

"One-one-seven Hunterhausen," Terry replied.

The answer cleared up nothing. "What's that supposed to mean?"

"It's the address for this house," he said.

I rang the doorbell and heard a buzz ring through the house. "So?" I asked. "What's special about that address?"

"It's the address for one of the houses we're supposed to visit for the story."

"One of the crazy houses?"

Before Terry could reply, there was a rattle at the door. It opened to reveal an elderly woman with a shapeless flowered dress and a tight bun of blue hair. Her brown eyes shifted back and forth between me and Terry. "Hidy," she said in a voice that was barely above a whisper. "What can I do for you?"

The woman looked sane enough. "We've got something of an emergency," I said. "Could we use your telephone?"

The woman pursed her lips. She ducked her head back into the house for a moment and looked left and right, then she emerged again and nodded. "All right," she whispered. "But you'll have to be quiet. They're sleeping."

"We'll be quiet as mice," I promised.

We followed the woman through a small living room. She tapped a finger to her lips then pointed to an open door. "The phone's in there," she whispered softly. "Be sure to be quiet."

"Thanks," I replied. The woman stayed near the front door as Terry followed me through the door into the kitchen. It was a warm, cheery room with gleaming oak floorboards and a yellow-checked tablecloth. There was an old round-topped fridge in the corner and a mustard-colored stove. Hanging right beside them was a red telephone with an old-fashioned dial.

"Okay," I said to Terry. "First I'm going to call nine-one-one and see if we can find a place to take Mr. Finley. Then I'm going to see if we can get hold of the coast guard."

Terry nodded. He held his camera up to his face and turned around slowly. "Should I start getting some shots for the story."

"No!" I shouted. Then I caught myself and lowered my voice. "Not yet. Let's get the rest of this mess off our hands before we start dealing with business. All right?"

Terry nodded, but he kept the camera to his eye. He appeared to be carefully framing a shot of a toaster. "Okay."

I picked up the phone and spun the dial through the emergency number. There was a click, then a momentary hum, then a series of rising tones. "We're sorry," said a recorded voice over the phone. "All circuits are busy now. Please try—" I hung up for a moment and tried again. This time there was only a fast busy signal. I dropped the phone on its cradle.

"I'm afraid we're going to need a phone book," I said.

There was a scream from the front room that made me jump a foot. Terry dropped his camera to the table with a crash. I rushed back through the door to find the woman standing on an ottoman. She looked down at me in terror.

"You woke them!" she cried. "You woke them!"

I looked around the room and saw no one. "Who?"

"The appliances!" she shouted. She pointed a quaking hand toward the silent television on the other side of the room. "They already got my little Dandelion. You better get up here quick, or they'll get you, too."

Terry came out of the kitchen with his camera clutched in ready to fire position. "What's going on?"

"Nothing," I said. "Go back into the kitchen and keep calling nine-one-one. See if you can get through."

Terry looked around the room for a moment, fired off a picture of the old woman standing on the ottoman, then retreated to the kitchen. I faced the woman and gave her what I hoped was a reassuring smile.

"Dandelion was your dog?" I asked.

"Yes," she replied with a sniff. "My poor little angel."

"And your dog was eaten by the refrigerator."

The woman's eyes widened, then narrowed in suspicion. "How did you know that?"

"I'm from the *Global Query*," I said, still smiling. "You called me on this phone this morning, remember?"

"*Global Query*," repeated the woman. She pursed her lips and shook her head slowly. "I don't remember anything about any *Global Query*."

"I talked to you myself, ma'am. You told me about the dog."

The woman seemed to consider this for a moment, then shook her head. "No," she said firmly. "You're with them. They were all sleeping, but you came in here and woke them up."

"I'm not with them. I came here because you called me."

"Liar," said the woman. "Liar, liar." Her voice took on the taunting tone of children in a school yard.

"Ma'am . . ."

"Button pusher!"

"Please, ma'am. I—"

"Toaster lover!"

I took a deep breath and gave it one last try. "We're not here to hurt you," I said quickly. "I'm going to go into the kitchen and get my friend, then we'll both get out of here and leave you alone."

The woman's eyes shifted left and right. "You're not with them?" she said in a rough whisper.

"No, we're not."

"Then you'd best be careful," warned the woman on the ottoman. "Those things are tricky—very tricky. You never know what they're going to do next."

"I'll be careful." I turned around to go back into the kitchen.

Then something struck me hard across the back of the head and I fell facedown on the floor.

FIVE

MY ASSAILANT WAS A CLOCK RADIO.

I lay there on the floor for a moment, staring into the blank face of the clock and listening to a high keening sound that seemed to come from somewhere just behind my ears. Only when an oversized TV remote bounced from the carpet beside my face did I find the energy to climb to my feet.

"You see," screamed Jean Myrtle. "Tricky, just like I said."

I turned around to face her. She was still standing on her ottoman, but now she held what looked like a calculator in her left hand. With a sharp gesture, she chucked the little machine my way. The pitch went wild and the device struck the wall several feet to my right. The case popped open as it hit the ground and dime-sized batteries rolled away across the floor.

"See there! It tried to bite you! Went right for your throat!"

"Yes, ma'am," I replied. "They're little, but they're mean." First a drunken ferry pilot and now a senile woman with a houseful of rebellious electronics. Locating nutcases was clearly one of my hidden talents. Mr. Genovese would have been pleased.

There was a warm feeling at the base of my skull. I reached back and felt around in my short blond hair. Sure enough, I felt a patch of something warm and sticky. When I pulled my hand around, it was streaked with blood. Looking at the scarlet stains on my fingers made me feel a little queasy. As scalp wounds go, this one was nothing to write home about, but anything that involves my blood escaping from my body is not my idea of a good time.

"I think it would be best if we leave," I said carefully.

Once again Mrs. Myrtle's brown eyes narrowed. "You're going to tell more of them, aren't you? You're going to bring a whole army of washers and dryers and curling irons to get me. I know you are!"

"Please, Mrs. Myrtle. I'm not helping them." With my toe I nudged the radio responsible for the dent in my skull. "You saw this one attack me. Doesn't that prove I'm on your side?"

This question called for more deep thought and a stream of mumbling. While our hostess considered the problem I backed away into the kitchen.

"How's the phone call coming?" I asked Terry.

Terry placed the phone back in its cradle and shrugged. "Not good," he replied. "All I get is a busy signal."

"Wonderful." I nodded toward the door. "Come on, we're getting out of here."

"Already?" Terry frowned. "Shouldn't we keep trying our phone call?"

"We can try somewhere else." I rubbed the back of my aching head. "I've already been hit by one appliance and had two near misses. If we stay around much longer, Mrs. Myrtle's aim might improve."

Terry reached over and grabbed my hand. "You're bleeding."

I shrugged. "I had a little argument with an AM/FM."

"You should put something on that." Terry spun a paper towel off a roll over the sink and handed it to me. "Direct pressure," he said. "That's best."

"Great." I took the paper and pressed it to the growing mound at the back of my skull. "Now let's get going."

"Aren't you going to interview Mrs. Myrtle for the article?" Terry asked. "I haven't even taken pictures yet."

"I think the only person that needs to interview Mrs. Myrtle is the county mental-health department. The woman is nuts."

"What about the refrigerator?" said Terry.

"What about it?"

"Aren't we even going to look inside," he asked. "You know, to see if it really did eat the dog?"

I turned and looked at the round-shouldered fridge. The idea that this heavy chunk of cast iron and freon could have chased down some little pooch was ludicrous. But then, Mrs. Myrtle had already shown that she wasn't above abetting her fantasies by a little direct intervention. If she was willing to throw a radio at me, might she have helped the refrigerator to do in her dog?

Checking the contents of the mad woman's cooler was not high on my list of things to do, and I certainly wasn't fond of the idea of finding a Pekingese mixed in with the frozen foods. The idea immediately brought an image I could have done without—a fuzzy little dog falling to the oak floor and shattering like a vase. But I advanced on the alleged dog-eating monster and took it by the handle.

Terry moved up beside me, his camera poised. "Just in case," he said.

I braced myself and pulled the freezer door open.

Nothing but casseroles and creamed vegetables stored to last out the ages in Tupperware of all shapes and sizes. There was no sign of a dog, and none of the burpable storage units looked big enough for even the scrawniest Chihuahua. "Looks like Dandelion isn't among the leftovers."

"What about the refrigerator part?" suggested Terry.

"She said freezer."

"Yeah, but—"

I held up a hand. "All right, I'll check." I took the handle on the bottom and pulled.

Immediately a streak of yellow shot from between shelves packed in milk and cheeselike products. A camera flash popped from over my shoulder, momentarily blinding me. My heart jumped in my chest as I waited for the sound of shattering canine. But the little dog did not break into a thousand pieces as it hit the ground. Instead it looked up at me with gratitude in its little brown eyes, gave one very cold whimper, then literally hightailed it away down the hall.

"Wow!" said Terry. "It really *was* in there."

"Did you get the shot?" I asked.

He nodded. "I think so."

"Good. Come on, we're out of here." My heart was still beating double time as I marched out of the kitchen and crossed the living room.

Mrs. Myrtle looked down on me from her Naugahyde perch. "Are you going to bring help?" she asked. Apparently she had decided we were on the side of the angels and not in league with the satans of circuitry.

"Absolutely," I said. I gave another of my reassure-the-Froot-Loop smiles. "We'll send someone right out." Someone with a nice big net and a snug white jacket.

"Make sure they bring peanut butter," she advised, her voice dropped to a conspiratorial whisper. "They *hate* peanut butter. Jams up their gears."

"I'll have them bring creamy and extra chunky just to be sure," I promised.

There was another burst from the camera flash. Terry hurried past me and took up a position near the door as he framed another shot. I grabbed him by the arm and dragged him outside.

"Come on, Terry. We can get more shots later." By my reckoning, I had more than enough material for our story on Mrs. Myrtle. If the rest of the phone calls led to places half as strange, the *Query* wouldn't have enough column inches to hold all the weirdness.

The rain had stopped. I took a deep breath of the cooling air and blew out a breath filled with frustration. It was going to be okay. I had come to Meridian to interview a group of nuts. I shouldn't be surprised that I had found one. All I had to do was relax, write my story, and dodge any flying radios. Everything else would take care of itself.

I turned toward the car and froze. "Terry?" I said slowly.

"Yeah?"

"How did my hood get open?"

Terry's only answer was to flash another picture.

"Stop that," I snapped. I ran toward the car and looked under the raised hood. Engines are not my strong point. In fact, I voluntarily confess that I don't know where the spark plugs lie, or even what the spark plugs do. However, I was pretty sure that there were not supposed to be a bunch of wires sticking up in the air.

Terry came up beside me and joined in staring at the engine. "Wow," he said.

For a moment genetics took over. Terry was a man. Surely that meant he had the ability to overhaul a carburetor and locate the business end of a dipstick— whatever that was. "Do you know what this means?" I asked hopefully.

He nodded. "Yeah."

"Great," I said in relief. "What is it?"

Terry shrugged. "Bad," he said. "It's bad."

I pressed my hands to my temples. There was a fierce headache growing behind my eyes. The recent collision between my skull and a small appliance had been enough to get it started, and the condition of my engine was giving it plenty of fuel. "I don't suppose you have any idea how to fix it?"

"No," said Terry. "Not really."

"Figures." I grabbed the edge of the hood and slammed it down. That's when I noticed that the passenger door was also open. I moved around, looked in the backseat, and gasped. "Finley is gone."

"The captain?" Terry stepped up to the window and looked at the empty seat. "Where do you think he went?"

I shook my head. "Maybe he went back to the docks." That's when I noticed a dark smear on the car seat. In the fading light, it looked black. The stain could have come from anything, but I was willing to bet it was blood.

"Is something wrong?" asked Terry.

"No." I shut the car door quickly. If Finley was hurt, we needed to get help as soon as possible.

I put my hands on my hips and turned slowly around. It was getting late and the light was fading quickly from the cloudy sky. From the hill where Mrs. Myrtle's house was perched, I could see fields and orchards spread out over the north end of the island. A few miles to the south were a tight cluster of buildings and the tall spire of a church. With the cap'n gone, and possibly injured, getting to civilization seemed like a really good idea.

"I don't know where Captain Finley went, but I know where we have to go," I said, pointing to the distant church. "It looks like the town is over that way. We still need to get to a phone, and that's our best bet."

Leaving the crippled car behind, we walked down the hill and headed toward the town. Terry walked easy and loose, eating up the ground in easy strides. His football days might be in the past, but there was no doubt that he was still fit. In the car, his size hadn't been so obvious. Now that we were walking side by side, the top of my head barely reached his shoulder. I was forced to take two steps for every one of his.

Mud splashed up over my shoes and onto my ankles. The winds shifted around to the north and began to blow in sharp chilly blasts. The gusts cut through the trees alongside the road with a whistling that went up and down the scale like a ten-year-old turned loose on a slide trombone. The temperature on the back side of the storms seemed to be at least twenty degrees colder than it had been before the rain started. I hugged my arms tight against myself and shivered as we hiked along the roadway toward what passed for downtown Meridian.

"What do you think is wrong with Mrs. Myrtle?" Terry asked.

"I'm not sure." Now that I was out of range of any vicious flying radios, my sympathy for Jean Myrtle was considerably stronger. "Whatever's wrong, she needs some help." The list of people that needed help was growing rapidly. As soon as we found a phone, I would have to inform the police of the wayward barge, the equally rambling ferry pilot, and the appliance-

phobic Mrs. Myrtle—not to mention poor Dandelion.

We crunched along the damp gravel road for what
had to be at least a mile. Ahead of us the last rays of
the sinking sun caught the top of the church steeple
and lit it like a torch. I was disappointed to see that it
looked no closer than it had when we started walking.
The light slipped away, and a chilly darkness settled
over Meridian.

According to the advertising, the brown pumps I
was wearing were supposed to have the sole of a
hiking boot, but the pain that was growing in my feet
did not agree. It felt more like the sole of a hardware
store. I stopped for a moment, shucked my right shoe,
and imitated a stork as I massaged my aching instep.
"Doesn't this seem strange to you?" I said.

"You mean Mrs. Myrtle?" asked Terry.

I shook my head as I slipped back into my right shoe
and shed my left. "Not just her. How many cars have
you seen since we got here?"

Terry thought for a moment. "Besides ours?"

"Yes, besides ours." I put the other shoe back on and
looked up and down the road. "There hasn't been a car
on this road since we got here. There are supposed to
be a couple hundred people on this island. Where are
they?"

"Maybe they got taken," suggested Terry. A light
came into his blue eyes and he leaned toward me with
excitement. "See, there was this town up in Alaska,
and everybody there just disappeared one day. This
guy came into the village the next day and found food

still on the tables and dogs waiting to be fed. It was a real mystery."

"What happened to them?"

Terry shrugged. "No one ever found out, but I think they were taken by aliens."

I closed my eyes and took a deep breath. It was a clear sign of encroaching exhaustion when I actually expected a reasonable response from Terry.

"Come on," I said. "Let's go see if the aliens left any food in town."

We had gone no more than a hundred yards farther when the air was suddenly torn by a loud, warbling cry. It came from somewhere ahead—somewhere close ahead.

Terry stumbled to a halt at my side. He raised his camera to his face and spun around like a gazelle out to make a portrait of an attacking lion. "What was that?" he asked in a hoarse whisper.

"I'm not sure," I replied. My heart thumped loudly against my ribs and I squinted into the shadowy forests that lined both sides of the road.

"It sounded like a wolf," said Terry. "Maybe we should walk the other way."

"Don't be ridiculous," I said firmly. "There aren't any wolves around here." This assertion sounded pretty good coming out of my mouth, but it didn't convince my own ears. The howl had matched the terrifying noise I remembered from a thousand old black-and-white movies. It made me think of Transylvanian castles and silver bullets.

The horrible sound came again. It was closer this

time, a long mournful cry that rose, paused, then rose again. It bypassed my brain completely and called up a knot of fear from the base of my spine. Suddenly flying radios seemed like a relatively minor hazard. "Come on," I said. "We're going back to Mrs. Myrtle's."

As I turned around I saw something moving in the trees on the left—a dark silhouette slipping from one trunk to the next. My breath froze in my chest. Branches snapped, and there was a sharp, barking sound.

Terry's hand reached out for mine and enclosed my fingers in a painfully tight grip. "What—" Before he could finish his question, a snarling came from the shadows. A dark form dashed between the trees and leaped onto the gravel road no more than a dozen feet away. The howl rose again, loud enough now that I found myself screaming in response.

There was a flash of brilliant white light that faded almost as quickly as it had come. Only after darkness had returned did I realize a couple of things: the flash of light had come from Terry's camera, and the thing on the road was a man. The afterimage burned into my eyes by that momentary flare and carried with it a vision of a round face, sandy hair, and glasses.

"What—" I stopped and took a deep breath. "What do you think you're doing?" I demanded.

The man in the road snarled at me. "Beware!" he said, "beware the wolf!" In the dim light I could see him pawing at the air with pale hands.

The headache that had been easing suddenly returned even stronger. I reached up and squeezed the bridge of my nose. "You're not a wolf."

"I *am* a wolf!" he said. There was a very unwolfish whining in his voice.

Terry's camera flashed again, glinting from the man's glasses. "He doesn't look like a wolfman," Terry said. "He doesn't even have a beard."

The would-be wolf started another howl.

"Stop that!" I shouted. I took a deep breath and let it out slowly. First the ferry captain, then Mrs. Myrtle, and now this wimpy wolfman. I had come to Meridian expecting to interview a town full of people who phoned in crazy, bogus stories, but it seemed that no one in Meridian was faking. I had landed on the Island of Dr. Dementia.

The howl cut off mid-warble. "Even a man who's pure at heart and . . . and . . ."

"Says his prayers at night," I finished. "I've seen the movie, but you're *not* a wolf."

The man gave a halfhearted snarl, whirled around, then ran back into the woods.

Terry stood in the center of the road, staring after him.

"Do you think he's really a werewolf?"

"No, of course not." I listened to the man crashing through the underbrush. Though he was certainly no monster, there was no doubt he was seriously disturbed. One nutcase might be happenstance, two was coincidence, but three was definitely becoming an asylum. I had no idea where all this insanity was coming from, but if three crazy people were wandering the outskirts of this island, there could be more hiding in the woods. And the next werewolf we ran into might be more convincing.

Suddenly I was very glad to have Terry with me. He might be gullible, but he was also very big and very strong.

"Come on," I said to him. "We need to get to town as soon as we can."

Despite my aching feet, we hurried down the road at a much faster pace. As we neared the town I was relieved to see the bright white glow of electric lights. It was good to know that something was still working in Meridian. Soon we could pass on the news of what we had seen and concentrate on getting off the island. But a hundred yards after I had first seen the lights, my hopes for a return to sanity faded.

There was a pickup truck sitting sideways across the road with both doors hanging ajar and a bucket of fried chicken spread across the front seat. Beyond it, a briefcase lay open on the gravel road. Loose papers fluttered around in the wind. As I bent down to examine the leather case, I heard crying. A figure dressed in a white gown ran across the road and was gone before either Terry or I could react.

"What was that?" asked Terry.

I shook my head. For the first time I was starting to feel really, deeply afraid. Something was seriously wrong in Meridian, Illinois. "Keep moving. The sooner we get to the police station the better."

Terry raised his camera and turned a slow circle in the middle of the street. "I really need my high-speed film," he said.

"Where is it?"

"Back in your car." He fired off a shot of the stalled truck. "You think we could—"

A blast of discordant organ notes came from the church on our right, followed by a high keening laugh. From somewhere not too far away, I heard a sharp crack. It might have been something falling, or the backfire from a car, but that wasn't what I suspected.

I grabbed Terry by the sleeve. "There's probably a store in town where you can get more film. Come on."

We passed a small restaurant where the tables had been turned upside down, then a pool hall with shattered windows. Terry snapped a few shots, but I was more intent on watching the dark windows of the buildings. All around us I could hear and feel movement. There were people here, maybe many people, but none of them were coming out to say hi. I walked close to Terry and hoped that his size would fool observers into thinking he was formidable.

Finally I spotted the sign I'd been hoping to see. I took Terry by the arm. "There's the police station. Come on."

We hurried across the deserted street and under the bright letters of the police station sign. Inside, there were a pair of desks, a single jail cell, and a rack on the wall holding at least a dozen shotguns and rifles.

At the desk in the back of the office a policeman sat hunched above a stack of paperwork. Relieved by the sight of his blue uniform, I hurried over to him.

"Officer, you need to—" That was as far as I got

before I realized that the policeman was not working on the papers, he was only bleeding on them. Or had been bleeding. From the bullet wound through his skull, I had no doubt that the officer was dead.

SIX

THE JIFFY MART BURNED WELL.

As I watched from our refuge inside Pete's Hardware and Auto Tire, the back of the convenience market split open and let out a jet of blue flames. I wondered how much of the fire was being fueled by greasy hotdogs and that yellow lard which passes for nacho sauce. The smoke probably carried more toxic substances than a nuclear meltdown, but all I could think about was the cupcakes, candy bars, and deep-fried potato wedges that were being wasted. I mourned them all.

"You want some more granola?" asked Terry. He held out a clear Baggie filled with a mixture that looked like sawdust spiced with a handfull of semi-petrified raisins.

I wanted to turn down his offer, but my stomach gave a growl more convincing than anything the wolfman on the road had managed. My lunch with Jimmy had not exactly come off as planned, and there had been little chance to eat anything since then. If I didn't get some serious calories into me soon, I thought I might go crazy myself. I dug into the bag of gritty granola and shoved a handful into my mouth.

When I was done, Terry tilted the bag to his lips and poured down the remainder. "Good thing I had this stuff in my pocket."

"Oh, yeah," I replied. I ran my tongue along my teeth to scrape off a coat of dry oat grit. "It's wonderful."

Terry shoved the empty bag into his pocket. "Aren't you going to sleep, Savvy?"

I shrugged. "I'm not sure that's a good idea. What if some bright boy gets the idea of setting fire to this place while I'm snoozing?"

Terry sighed. "I wish we could go home," he mumbled. For the moment the excitement of going on a field assignment seemed to have vanished. He had dutifully snapped pictures of the dead policeman, but the sight of the body had obviously left him more than a little rattled. I couldn't really blame him.

"You and me both," I replied. "But we're just going to have to stick around till we can figure out what to do next."

After finding the dead policeman, Terry and I had tried every phone in the station. They were all as dead as the officer. The police radio had been the victim of a serious assault with intent to turn it into rubble. Communication between Meridian and the rest of the world was completely cut off.

We had found the open door of Pete's Hardware while looking for another place to make a call. The phones in the store were just as defunct as those at the police station, but at least at Pete's there was a blessed lack of corpses. It also contained the essense of life itself: clean rest rooms and a soda machine.

For six hours we had watched the town through the blinds over the store window. So far, none of the crazies wandering the streets of Meridian had taken an interest in Pete's, but I couldn't be sure that the armistice would continue.

"I can watch the place while you sleep," Terry volunteered. "Then you watch it while I sleep."

I looked into his face for a moment. Terry was gullible, but surely he wasn't so gullible that he'd let someone walk over and torch the building without waking me. "All right," I said at last. "You stay here and watch until"—I checked my watch—"three A.M. Then I'll take over till six. By then it should be daylight."

Terry nodded in agreement. "Okay," he said. "I'll see you at three."

I walked down the aisle of the store. Between the cans of paint and boxes of nails, I saw little that offered a comfortable place to nap. Finally I dragged a sack of tarpaulins from a high shelf and spread one of the heavy cloths on the floor. Another I wadded together to make a crude pillow. Then I kicked off my muddy pumps and lay down.

Tired as I was, I had a hard time falling asleep. I lay there in the dark, trying one explanation after another to rationalize the circumstances in Meridian. Nothing seemed to fit. It was difficult for me to think of anything that could leave an entire town in such a condition. Maybe there was a state psychiatric facility somewhere on the island from which the lunatics had all escaped. Or maybe what was happening was some unique form of mass hysteria. Maybe it was a full moon.

Whatever the cause of the madness, I wasn't likely to solve it lying on my back in a hardware store. I rolled over on my side, closed my eyes, and tried to let go of the problem long enough to catch a little sleep. But just as I was starting to slip into an exhausted doze, a new image appeared in front of me.

It wasn't a vision of madness or danger, but in its own way it was just as frightening. What I saw was a clear image of Jimmy Knoles, dressed in a crisp blue suit and old-school tie, chatting with some fawning female admirer.

I sat up in the darkness. Here I was, cold, hungry, and bunking on the floor in the middle of an islandful of loonies, while Jimmy crashed in some warm hotel room and snacked down on Brie and little cocktail weenies. For the first time I began to wonder if he had another reason for being glad that I wasn't going to the conference. Maybe he hadn't been worried about getting closer to me, maybe he was worried about me seeing him getting closer to someone else. After all, the conference was going to be full of reporters, some of whom Jimmy had known for years. He had probably made a connection with some old flame and wanted to keep me safely out of the picture.

For the next two hours I tossed and turned on the floor. Several times I fell into an uneasy drowse, but every time I came out of it with a new vision of

Jimmy's smiling face. As each of these half-formed dreams succeeded the other, the dress worn by the admirer was cut a little lower and fit a little tighter. Long before three, I gave up on getting any rest and rejoined Terry at the front door.

"See anything?"

He shook his head without looking away from the window. "The space guy walked by a minute ago. I haven't seen anybody else for a long time."

The space guy was Terry's name for a man wearing a shiny metal bowl on his head and holding something that appeared to be a concoction of coat hangers and aluminum foil. The man had walked by twice shortly after we had taken up our base in the hardware store, but he hadn't seemed to notice us—or much of anything else.

"Why don't you try getting some sleep?" I suggested. "I'm not having any luck at it."

"Okay," Terry said immediately. "I'm pretty tired." He stood up and stretched, then turned toward the back of the store.

Halfway to the makeshift bed, he stopped and turned back toward me. "Savvy?"

"Yeah?"

"Do you know what's wrong with all the crazy people?"

I shook my head. "No."

"What are we going to do in the morning?"

"We're going to hope things make more sense," I said. "And we're going to find a way off this island."

Terry stood silently for a moment. "What if it's a disease?" he said at last.

"The craziness?"

He nodded. "What if it's something like a bad cold, or maybe the flu, only this kind of flu makes you go crazy?"

I readied a quick answer, then swallowed it. Something decidedly odd was going on in Meridian, and after all, we were living in the age of strange infectious diseases. With all the nasty things that were floating around, who was to say that there wasn't such a thing as brain flu?

"You could be right," I said. "I've never heard of any disease like that, but I've never heard of anything else that could make a whole town go insane. Maybe it *is* a disease."

For a moment Terry's face was split by a proud smile and I was favored by a visit from the great dimples. Then his smile crumpled. "Can we catch it?" he asked.

I was definitely going to have to reassess my view of Terry. He might not always seem to have all eight cylinders firing, but he was obviously thinking harder than I had given him credit.

"If it is a disease," I said, "then I guess it's possible that we can catch it. But I don't think we should worry about that yet. Our first job is to keep ourselves out of trouble and let someone know what's going on here."

Terry nodded. "All right." He turned and shuffled back to the makeshift bed.

Apparently the difficulty of the situation was not enough to prevent Terry from snoozing. Within ten seconds of hitting the ground, his snores were ringing down the aisle. For the next three hours I sat by the front door and watched the Jiffy Mart turn into a stack of smoking concrete blocks. I saw the space guy again, complete with his handheld contraption, walking between two buildings on the other side of the road. Sometime after five I spotted someone else moving with a stumbling, jerky walk across the parking lot of the church.

As dawn approached, the town seemed to settle down. I held my hand over my mouth to stifle frequent yawns as the distant noises of shouts and screams faded. The fire burned out. The sun rose in a sky that was blessedly empty of clouds and rain. As the sky grew pink I lowered my head, just to rest my eyes a moment or two.

"Is it six yet?" Terry suddenly asked.

I jumped awake and saw that it was full daylight. The main street of Meridian lay empty and bright under yellow sunshine. I glanced down at my watch. "It's closer to eight."

"What do we do now?"

Before I could come up with a reply, two men appeared from up the street. One was tall, with a neatly trimmed red beard and a tan baseball cap on his head. He wore a light jacket against the cool morning air and carried a clipboard in one hand. The second man was much shorter, with round-rimmed glasses and a tight, worried look. The two men stopped in front of the Jiffy Mart and talked with each other. The taller man took out his clipboard and wrote something. It was hard to be sure without watching—maybe they were discussing the price of pigs on Mars—but neither of them appeared to be nuts.

I opened the lock on the door. "Let's go talk to these guys," I said.

Terry put his hand over mine. "You better let me go first. They might be crazy."

I shrugged. "Tell you what, we'll go together. We need a boat to get out of this place, and I don't have any idea where to find one. If these guys are nuts, then we run for it. Deal?"

"Sure," said Terry. He flexed his arms and I saw an impressive array of muscles ripple under his shirt.

There was a sudden sharp smell of testosterone in the room. Terry might be a mild-mannered UFO loving photographer, but he was also an ex-jock. I had a suspicion that if we found trouble, getting Terry to actually run away from it might be a problem.

"Remember," I said. "We're going to talk to them. Calmly. Right?"

"Sure."

Terry headed back down the aisle to collect his camera gear. Without waiting for him, I cautiously pushed open the door of the hardware store. The men in the street spun around and looked my way, but neither of them made a move to come closer.

"Hello," I called to them.

The bearded man nodded. "Hello," he replied slowly. "Tell me, how are you feeling this morning?"

"Tired," I said. "But all right. I don't suppose either one of you can tell me what's going on around here?"

The two men exchanged glances. "You really all right?" said the shorter man.

"Yes." I stepped away from the door and took a few steps into the street. The two men held their ground, but I could see that my approach was making them nervous. "What about you?"

Red beard passed the clipboard to the man with glasses, then took a step toward me and stretched out his hand. "I'm Jordan Cullison."

I took his hand. "Savannah Skye," I said, giving the byline I used at the *Query*. The false name always made me feel a little dishonest, but it had its advantages.

Cullison nodded. "I don't recognize you, Ms. Skye. Are you a visitor to our island?"

I couldn't help but smile. "Yes. It looks like I picked the wrong day to visit."

"I think you could say that," agreed Cullison. He returned my smile, revealing a bright line of white teeth above his ruddy whiskers.

Terry chose that moment to come out the door. "Are you okay, Savvy?"

At once Cullison pulled his hand from mine and stepped back. "Who are you?" he demanded. His right hand dropped into the pocket of his light jacket.

I had no idea if the pocket contained a pistol, a knife, or only a spare pen, but I moved quickly to step between the two men. "This is Terry Banyon. He works with me."

Cullison slowly drew his hand away from his pocket. "What about you, Mr. Banyon, are you feeling all right?"

Terry looked a little confused, but at least he managed a nod. "Sure," he said. "I'm okay."

The man in the round glasses decided to join the party. "What are you two doing over here?" he asked.

His manner was more than a little bossy. He looked back and forth between us as if he expected an answer and expected it quick. Considering the circumstances, and my lack of a decent night's sleep, his attitude did not endear him to me.

"Are you the mayor?" I replied.

"No," said the man. He stood stiffly and tilted his nose into the air. "I'm *Doctor* Frederick Benedict." The way he said "doctor" held just enough extra emphasis to let me know that he considered this word the most important part of his name. Behind his thick glasses, his hazel eyes studied me. Evidently he wanted to see that I was properly impressed. "I'll ask again, what are you doing here?"

I was in no mood to be intimidated by a country doctor. "Well, Fred," I replied, "I'm a reporter and Terry here is my photographer." I reached into my shoulder bag, withdrew a small recorder, and held it toward the short man's face. "Do you have any comment about the recent events in Meridian?"

In my experience, half the doctors in the world are so worried about malpractice suits that they wouldn't give a reporter an opinion on the color of the sky. The other half are complete hams. Give them a chance, and they'll not only give you a ten-minute discourse on why water is wet, they'll also take credit for inventing it.

I had expected Benedict to be in the ham squad, but he came down on the shy side of the line. He pulled back from the recorder as if it was a loaded gun. "What events?" he asked.

I smiled. After a night of cowering in the dark, it

was good to have someone to badger. Benedict had to know something about what was going on, and I was going to find out what. "Come now, Doctor. I'm sure you must have seen something unusual last night."

It was Cullison who answered. "What did you see, Ms. Skye?"

I turned the recorder his way. "I'm sorry, Mr. Cullison. What is your position here?"

He smiled. "It happens that I am the mayor of Meridian. Also head of the street department, water department, chief cook, and bottle washer." Cullison paused and hooked his thumbs into the belt loop of his jeans. "This is a small town, Ms. Skye, and it's had a very rough day. If you have any information about what's happened here, I'd suggest you give it to us."

The reversal of who was asking the questions and who was giving the answers caught me by surprise. "I don't have any answers," I replied. "We came out here yesterday because we heard that something was going on in Meridian. Since we got here, we've seen—"

"Crazy people," interrupted Terry.

Cullison shifted his attention to Terry. "Can you give me an example?"

Terry nodded enthusiastically. "There was the ferry driver, and Mrs. Myrtle, and the wolf guy, and the space guy." He ticked them off on his fingers as he went. Then he paused and shook his head. "And a whole bunch more."

The mayor watched Terry for a few seconds, perhaps hoping that he was going to explain something about the people on the list. But Terry only stared back at him. "I see," Cullison said at last. He turned back to me. "Are you certain he's all right?"

"He's as fine as he gets," I said. "Now, do you have any idea what's going on?"

The mayor shook his head. "I'm afraid I don't remember anything of the last two days," he said.

"Nothing?" That idea seemed as crazy as anything I had seen. "How can you remember nothing about two whole days?"

"Believe me," said Cullison, "it's as much a mystery to me as it is to you."

"I also remember nothing," added Dr. Benedict.

Something about the way Benedict moved his hands made me look at him more closely. "You seem familiar to me, Doctor. Have we met?"

The doctor pursed his lips for a moment, then shook his head. "I don't believe I've seen you before, and I have quite a good memory for faces."

"I know who he is," said Terry.

I glanced over at him in surprise. "You do?"

Terry nodded. "He's the space guy."

Once Terry said it, Dr. Benedict's secret identity was obvious. The arrogant doctor was indeed the wandering loony we had seen during the night.

Apparently, Benedict was not flattered by the nickname. "I don't know what you're talking about."

"Terry and I saw you several times last night, Doctor. You were walking around town with a metal salad bowl on your noggin and a wad of junk in your hand." I held up my recorder. "Care to comment on that."

Benedict pushed my hand back and turned his face

away. "That's ridiculous. I would never behave in such a fashion."

Mayor Cullison put his hand on the shorter man's shoulder. "I don't know, Doc. It fits with what we've seen from other folks." He looked back at me. "We need to discuss this, Ms. Skye. Would you and your colleague mind coming along with us to the police station?"

I shook my head. "We'll come. We need to get to the bottom of this ourselves." As the group turned down the street I had another thought. "Has someone moved the body?"

Both Cullison and Benedict froze in their tracks. "What body?" they asked together.

"At the police station," I said. "Terry and I found it last night."

Cullison lifted the tan baseball cap from his head and ran a shaking hand through his red hair. "Someone's dead at the police station?"

I nodded. "One of the policemen. Or at least, he was wearing a police uniform. We found him sitting at his desk, but he had been shot in the head."

"Perhaps he was only injured," Dr. Benedict suggested. "After all, not all cranial wounds result in death. I sincerely doubt you have the medical experience to judge such circumstances, Ms. Skye."

The arrogance of the statement raised my hackles again. "How much experience do you need to recognize dead?"

Mayor Cullison sighed and jammed his hat back into place. "It must be Tom Macavoy. He's the only officer in Meridian that has a uniform. Come on. Let's go see to him."

The police station was only two doors down, and we made the trip quickly. I held back as Cullison and Dr. Benedict went inside.

"Aren't we going in?" asked Terry.

I shook my head. "Not unless we have to. I've already seen all I want of that particular body."

Terry peered over my head. "Maybe I should go. I only took a couple of pictures last night because it was so dark. The light will be better now. Mr. Genovese will probably want more shots."

He started to step past me, but I took him by the arm. "Stay here," I said. "If Bill Genovese wants to start running pictures of bodies in the *Query,* he can come take them himself."

Ten seconds later a voice called from inside. "Ms. Skye, could you step inside please?"

It was my turn to sigh. "Looks like I'm not going to get any choice." I went through the door and found Dr. Benedict waiting for me with a scowl on his face and his arms folded across his narrow chest.

"Well," said the doctor. "Where is this body you told us about?"

I pointed toward the back of the office. "Right over—" I stopped in midsentence. The desk where the dead policeman had been sitting was now decorated by a neat stack of folders and a single yellow apple. I walked back to it with my mouth hanging open. The cheap pinewood was polished and clean under the folders. There was no blood, and certainly no body.

Mayor Cullison watched me from across the room. "Are you sure about what you saw?"

"He was here," I insisted. "He was lying across this desk, and there was blood everywhere."

Behind me I heard Dr. Benedict give a derisive snort. "Maybe *I'm* not the one that was crazy last night."

SEVEN

"IT SEEMS YOUR DEAD MAN IS QUITE LIVELY," SAID DR. Benedict. He got up from the floor and brushed dust away from the knees of his pale gray chinos. "I see no evidence that there was ever any blood on or around the desk." His tone included an unsaid but very clear "you idiot."

I shook my head. "I saw it. We both saw it."

"I'm sure you did," said Jordan Cullison. He walked slowly around the room with his hands clasped at his back. "Or thought you did."

My molars ground together so loudly, I was certain everyone in the room could hear. "I didn't *think* I saw a dead policeman in this room, I did see a dead policeman. Terry even took pictures."

"Really?" The doctor turned to Terry. "May I see these pictures?"

Terry pointed at his camera. "They're not developed yet."

"Of course," said Benedict. "How handy."

I was the one who had worried about keeping Terry calm, but it was my blood that was starting to boil. "Let me tell you something, Doc. You can take your—"

Cullison held up a hand. "Please, Ms. Skye." He looked from me to Terry and sighed. "Maybe you two saw a body, and maybe not. I'm convinced you thought there was something unusual in this room. But let me tell you what I saw last night."

I crossed my arms over my chest. "I thought you didn't see anything. I thought you didn't remember anything for the last two days."

The mayor winced and looked away. "I'm afraid that wasn't quite the truth. The fact is, I saw plenty of things in the last forty-eight hours—it's just that none of them made sense."

I studied Cullison's face as he spoke. The mayor of Meridian had the rugged good looks of a lumberjack, and there was an appealing warmth in his brown eyes. It was easy to see how he had been elected. "Did you see people acting crazy?" I asked.

He drew in a deep breath and shook his head. "Not quite. I think *I* was one of the crazy people."

"You?"

Cullison opened his mouth to say something, closed it, then started again. "Let me back up. Wednesday was the annual Apple Festival."

I nodded. "The ferry pilot said something about the festival."

"He probably had some extra business the last

couple of days. The festival is a big deal on the island," said Cullison. "Apples are our largest crop, and the economy of Meridian is tied very closely to the success or failure of the crop. So every year, when the harvest comes in, we have a celebration. It's a time when all the families on the island get together, play a little softball, drink a little beer, and eat a lot of apples."

The mayor resumed his pacing, circling slowly past the desk where Terry and I had found the body of the dead policeman. "Practically every resident of Meridian who's able to get out of bed shows up at the festival. Wednesday, we had one of the best crowds in years." His voice had a wistful quality, as if he were talking about something that had happened years ago, not three days. "I judged the apple-pie contest, and ran in the three-legged race, and played softball against a team from the high school. That softball game's the last thing I remember before the samurai."

The last word made me cough in surprise. "What did you say?"

"A samurai," repeated Cullison. "You know, an ancient Japanese warrior with a long sword and padded armor?"

I nodded. "I know what a samurai is, I'm just waiting for you to tell me what one was doing at an apple festival in the middle of the Mississippi River."

"Chasing me," said the mayor. "The way I remember it, the samurai showed up in the long grass beyond left field, right along the third-base line." Cullison stopped pacing, his brown eyes focused on something in the distance. "He rode a huge gray horse, a real monster. It smashed right through the apple-bobbing tent, and ran across the grass with sod flying out from its hooves. It came straight for me."

"It couldn't have been real," I said.

Cullison shrugged. "It was real to me. The samurai chased me to my car, then stayed right on my tail all the way to my home. All night long I hid under the bed while he stomped around. I could hear him, I could see him. It was real."

There was a low whistle at my back. I turned around and saw that Terry had joined us in the station. His blue eyes were fixed on Cullison. "Wow," he said. "You got the crazy disease."

The term caught Dr. Benedict's attention. "What disease would that be?"

Before Terry could launch into a ten-minute explanation, I gave a fast summary. "Terry has a theory that all the people going nuts around here have caught some kind of disease."

I expected the doctor to reject this idea immediately. Instead he rubbed his chin and nodded slowly. "There are many diseases which can alter perceptions of reality. Though I find it hard to believe that so many people could have contracted any ailment so rapidly."

Terry leaned past me and looked at the clean desk. "Where's the dead guy?"

"Did you also see a dead police officer?" asked Cullison.

"Yeah," Terry said with a nod. He raised a finger and pointed at the desk. "He was right here."

Cullison turned and looked at Dr. Benedict. "Their stories agree."

Benedict shrugged. "It means nothing. The event was hours ago, and they've been together ever since. If they were in a state of delusion, it would be totally unremarkable for them to have shared impressions."

"We didn't share anything but a hiding place," I said. "The policeman was here."

Benedict gave me a smile as warm as Antarctica. "Then where is he?"

I returned his smile with one of my own. One thing was sure, when I wrote this up for the paper, Benedict was not going to come off well. "You tell me. Shouldn't a policeman be on duty here?"

"She has a point," said Cullison. "Where is Tom?"

"He could be anywhere," said Benedict. "There was a lot of trouble on this island in the last couple of days, and I expect Officer Macavoy is simply off attending to his job." He tapped his finger against the clean desk. "We have no evidence here that anyone has been killed."

Terry stumbled toward the table with his mouth hanging open. "You mean there was no dead guy?"

"Of course there—" I began.

"Exactly," cut in Benedict. "There's been no murder."

"Me and Savvy must have caught the crazy disease," said Terry. "And we didn't even know it."

"That's a strong possibility," agreed the doctor.

I wondered just how many synonyms I could find for *quack*. "Fine," I said. "You keep on believing that. In the meantime I'll find the body."

"Oh," said Benedict with his irritating smile, "do you also have police experience?"

Mayor Cullison moved between us. "Please," he said. "We've no idea what has happened to the town over the last couple of days. If everyone was affected as we were, there could be some folks in real danger around here. Others may not have recovered from whatever is causing this."

"We'll help in any way we can," I said quickly.

"I appreciate the offer, Ms. Skye," said the mayor. "But perhaps the best thing to do is get you off the island right away. If some people are still . . . unbalanced, we can't risk anyone getting hurt."

I shook my head. "We're journalists. We're used to danger."

"We are?" Terry's eyes had gone wide.

I glared at him. "Yes. We are." Mr. Genovese had sent me to this place to follow up on a series of phone calls. He had probably expected it to turn out to be nothing but coincidence, but now that it looked like there was going to be a real story after all, I wanted to be in the middle of it.

Aid came from an unexpected quarter. "It may be better if they do stay," said Dr. Benedict.

"Why?" asked the mayor. "No offense, Ms. Skye, I know you're only trying to do your job. But we've got enough on our hands without watching out for a reporter."

Dr. Benedict moved closer to me, his hazel eyes studying my face from behind the thick round lenses of his glasses like an entomologist examining the wings of a fly. "The fact is, we can't allow them to leave. If there actually is a disease, they might transport it off the island. They have to stay here until we're certain we understand what's happening."

Cullison frowned. "All right. Then our first job has to be finding a way to contact some outside authority. We need to get the state boys in here as fast as we can."

"We'll have to be cautious," Benedict warned. "If there *is* a disease, and it's contagious, we want to expose as few people as we can. If we bring in dozens of state police, they might only serve to spread the disease to other areas."

The statement reminded me of something I had been meaning to ask. "Is there any way onto the island other than by ferry?"

"No," said the mayor. "There's a plan to build a bridge, but that's years away. Right now the *Silver Belle*'s the only way on or off the island."

I winced. "Then there might be a problem."

Both Benedict and Cullison stared at me. "What's wrong?" asked the mayor.

"It's the ferry. It's sort of . . . well, sort of gone."

"What do you mean, gone?" demanded Dr. Benedict. "This may be nothing but more of your personal delusions. Ferries do not simply vanish in a puff of smoke."

"This is no dream," I snapped back. "The ferry drifted away, or floated off, or sailed for China. Choose any term you like. The ferry pilot passed out on the way over here. I managed to land the thing, but it drifted away once Terry and I got off."

"Obviously the concept of a mooring rope is beyond your grasp," said the doctor.

"Hey," said Terry. "Stop picking on her." It was not a particularly elegant speech, but it was obviously heartfelt. Terry stepped toward the doctor with an uncharacteristic scowl on his face.

Though Terry stood at least a foot taller than Benedict, the doctor did not seem the least bit intimidated. "Touch me, and I'll sue your paper for all it's worth." His forehead creased in thought. "What paper do you two work for, anyway?"

I gave myself a moment to try and think of some impressive journal, or some way to place my less than illustrious place of business in a better light. Terry didn't hesitate.

"We work for the *Global Query*," he declared proudly.

Mayor Cullison frowned. "I thought you two were from the *Post-Dispatch*. What's the *Global Query*? Is that a Chicago paper?"

"I'll tell you what it is," said Benedict. He looked at me and chuckled. "This *Query* of theirs is one of those miserable rags which take up space in the supermarket aisles. They run nothing but stories on angels and grapefruit diets."

"Is that right?" asked Cullison.

I shrugged. "The *Query* is a national weekly. We run

stories on a variety of subjects." It was the standard answer that Bill Genovese gave in defending the paper, and as always it was not exactly convincing.

The mayor frowned heavily, his lips disappearing behind a bristle of beard. "I didn't know you were from a tabloid."

"Does it make a difference?"

"It does to me," said Cullison. "I don't want this town's troubles being turned into some sensational story."

I glanced at the smirking Benedict and thought of new terms for *ugly* and *arrogant* and *runt*. "I don't think you're going to have a choice about sensationalism. You've got a whole town going nuts out here. That's not exactly the kind of story that gets buried on page seventeen. As soon as this leaks to television, you're going to have three dozen news helicopters circling overhead."

Cullison's chin dropped down to his chest. He pulled a chair away from the desk and sat down heavily. "Meridian's not ready for this," he said softly. Once again he lifted his baseball hat and ran his hands through his red hair. "I'm not ready. I'm just a tractor salesman who picked up a hundred votes on a rainy Tuesday."

I walked closer to him. "Mayor, just because I work for the *Query,* don't assume I'm a hack. If you cooperate with me, I'll write the best, most objective story you could hope for."

Benedict laughed again. "Where did you get your objective-journalism training, interviewing circus freaks?"

"Mayor," I said, ignoring the gibe from the doctor. "You said we needed to get in touch with the authorities. Is the telephone system out everywhere?"

"As far as I can tell."

"And the radio here is destroyed." I pointed across the room at the shattered electronics littering a table. "That's one thing about last night I know wasn't an illusion. So, where do we go from here?"

Dr. Benedict shoved past me and headed for the door. "I know where I'm going," he said. "The medical clinic may be completely unattended. If there's anyone injured, they very likely will come to the clinic for care. I should be there to help them."

Cullison nodded. "You're right, Doc. You ought to go on to the clinic . . . and be careful, you don't have any idea what you'll run into."

Benedict gave a last nod to the mayor. He looked at me for a moment and gave a grunt of laughter. Then he turned and vanished through the door.

"Is he always so rude?" I asked.

The mayor's smile flashed brightly above his red beard. "Doc's not rude, he's a genuine asshole."

I couldn't help but laugh. "And I thought I was the only one that noticed."

"Hardly. Benedict's only been in town for six months, and already he's managed to tick off most of the long-timers." Cullison rocked forward in his chair and leaned his elbows against his knees. "But, he's a doctor, and he was willing to relocate here. That makes him a very valuable man."

"What now?" I asked.

The mayor jerked his thumb toward the door. "No matter what I think of Benedict, he's got the right idea. I need to get out there and see how the people in this town are doing. If that means going door-to-door, that's what I'm going to do."

I thought back over the story that the mayor had told. "Where was this Apple Festival?"

"At the fairgrounds. It's a mile or two north of here."

"If that's where you started having hallucinations, it might be connected to what's going on in Meridian. Maybe that's the place to start."

Cullison thought about it for a moment, then slowly nodded. "As long as we get started." He stood up and put his cap back in place. "I've got a car a couple of blocks north. Let's go."

"You've decided to let us come along?"

He nodded. "I don't know that I can stop you, so I might as well have you where I can see you."

It was an attitude that I wished every public official would share. We followed Cullison out of the silent police station and down the empty street to a waiting four-wheel-drive wagon. Terry shared the backseat with the box of parts from a John Deere tractor while I took the shotgun seat. Seen in the daylight, it was still obvious that something was wrong with Meridian. Not only was there a conspicuous lack of traffic, but a considerable amount of trash had been spread across the lawns of the town.

One front yard boasted a pile of white rubble. It took me a few moments to realize that it was the shattered remains of a plaster deer. Another yard held a child's plastic swimming pool that was crumbled under the weight of an aluminum fishing boat. At a third house, dozens of shoes stretched across the porch, marched down the stairs, and extended along the sidewalk to the road in a neatly arranged line.

"Everybody must have had the crazy disease," Terry said as he looked through the window.

Watching the quiet town, I had to admit that Terry's disease theory was seeming ever more plausible. Nothing else seemed to fit the kind of chaos that had struck Meridian.

As we approached the fairgrounds I noticed a trio of cars smashed together in the road. They were an oddly assorted group, with a rusty pickup at the back of the pileup, a dark sedan in the center, and a gleaming Mercedes convertible at the front of the line. Cullison brought his wagon to an abrupt halt and ran along the cluster of vehicles. All were empty.

The mayor stopped by the convertible and ran his hand along the crumpled fender. The little car had taken a heavy shot from the sedan. It had been knocked sideways across the road. The whole driver's side of the vehicle had the texture of a soggy waffle. The air bag on the car had obviously inflated on impact and the open roof had let the leather seats fill with rain. But I could see no blood or any other sign of the driver. A soft, insistent chime sounded over and over, to remind the vanished owner that they had left behind their keys.

"This is Jenny Franklin's car," said Cullison, and

shook his head. "She just moved to the island a few days ago."

If she was a newcomer, it was clear she was a rich newcomer. I recognized the convertible as a model whose starting price was somewhere above that of the average house.

"It's probably a good sign that no one's here," I said. "If these people felt good enough to get out of their cars and go somewhere else, then they couldn't be too badly hurt." I said it to reassure Cullison, and it seemed to work, but I wasn't very sure of the words myself. The chiming of the car's electrical system in the middle of the silent road was eerie—like an abandoned child crying for its mom.

We climbed back into Cullison's wagon and maneuvered around the wreck. Five minutes later we turned onto the road to the fairgrounds.

"Wow," said Terry.

I nodded. "Yeah. Wow."

It looked like a tornado had been there ahead of us. Tents had been torn and scattered over the green grass. Trash was spread up and down the road, including hundreds of crumpled paper cups and hundreds more brown apple cores. Banners and streamers had been pulled down from trees and fences and left to tangle on the ground. Booths where local civic organizations had run mild forms of gambling disguised as games of skill had been toppled on their sides or broken into stacks of scrap lumber. Pounded by the heavy rains during the previous day, whole fields had turned into muddy stews of half-eaten apples, colored paper, and more than a few articles of clothing.

Cullison stopped his car near the end of the road and we all piled out. Despite the disaster on the field, we shared the parking area with better than a dozen cars and trucks. Many fairgoers had apparently chosen to leave the place on foot.

Terry hurried away from the car, the electric motors of his camera sending a steady stream of whines as he fired off shots of the disaster. I stuck close to Cullison as he walked the edge of the fairgrounds.

"I can't believe it," said the mayor. His voice was shaky and he seemed near tears. "Everyone was here—laughing, having fun. How can so little time make such a difference?"

"Bad things always seem to happen in a hurry," I replied. "This place is a mess, but it's only paper and trash. Things could be a lot worse."

"I guess," Cullison agreed, but he didn't sound too sure. He wandered away, kicking at the heaps of damp rubbish.

I bent down and picked up an apple. A single large bite had been taken from one side, leaving a puckered brown patch, but the rest of the fruit was smooth and shiny gold. As I turned it over in my hand I had a sudden memory of the ferry pilot munching an apple during the crossing.

"Savvy!" Terry suddenly called from behind us.

I turned my head and saw him looking down at something on the ground. At once my stomach pulled tight. I tossed the partially eaten apple and hurried back toward Terry, my shoes squishing on the damp ground. Cullison ran past me, his long legs carrying him to the place where Terry stood. The mayor looked down for a moment, then spun away.

As I drew closer I saw that Terry was standing over a stack of red, white, and blue streamers mixed with boards marked with the all-American word BINGO. The heap of trash looked like any of a dozen that littered the field, except this heap had legs.

"My God," Cullison muttered. He pulled in a shaky breath and tilted his head back.

I knelt down beside the pile. The legs that protruded from the heap were smooth, tan, and hairless—a young woman's legs. As I began moving the banners out of the way, I uncovered black gym shorts, a patch of bare midriff showing an admirably flat tummy, an abbreviated gold T-shirt, and hands with nails painted in green nail polish. Finally I exposed a girl's face topped with short, spiky dark hair. A smear of fluorescent-pink lipstick remained on her face and streaks of mascara ran back from the corners of her eyes. At a first guess, I put her age at around nineteen.

"That's Jenny Franklin," said Cullison. "It was her car that was wrecked out on the road." The mayor swallowed hard and shook his head. "Jenny grew up around here. I used to work for her father at the docks over in Illinois. How am I ever going to tell him about Jenny? What am I going to say?"

I put a hand on the girl's forehead and smoothed back her spiky hair. "You can tell him you saved her."

Cullison blinked in surprise. "What?"

"She's alive," I said.

Right on cue, the girl opened her eyes. She flailed around, delivering a backhanded blow that caught me on my cheek and knocked me on my rear.

"Elephants!" she screamed. "Stop the elephants!"

EIGHT

"THE GREEN ONES," JENNY FRANKLIN INSISTED. "THE GREEN ones are the worst."

The girl sat huddled in the back of Mayor Cullison's car with a muddy denim jacket thrown over her shoulders. Every now and then a tremor ran through her body, shaking her like a rag doll. Since we picked her up from the soggy fairgrounds and eased her over to the car, she had said very little, and what she did say made no sense.

I shoved the tractor parts out onto the grass and sat down in the backseat with my arm around the shivering girl. The seat of my pants was uncomfortably damp from my impromptu sit-down in the muddy field, but there wasn't much I could do about it. Outside, Mayor Cullison and Terry searched the ruined fairgrounds for any other survivors. So far, they had turned up nothing but spoiled food and wet paper.

"Watch out!" the girl cried suddenly.

"It's going to be all right," I said.

Jenny trembled against me, her breath coming in fast, shallow gasps. "The green ones sneak up on you," she whispered.

"Green elephants?"

"Elephants?" The girl rolled her eyes and snorted, her voice gaining volume. She gave a convulsive jerk. "Everyone knows there's no such thing as green elephants!"

"No, of course not."

Jenny's blue eyes darted left and right before settling on my face. She leaned forward, placing her upturned nose within an inch of mine. "It's the green tigers," she said. "Those are the ones you have to look out for."

Just then Mayor Cullison splashed across the muddy field and looked in through the car door, his face creased with concern. "I don't see anyone else around the fairgrounds."

"I think we should get Jenny to the clinic as soon as possible," I replied.

"I thought you said she wasn't injured."

"She's not, as far as I can tell. She's scratched up, but she is still having something of a problem."

"Yellow!" shouted Jenny Franklin. "Yellow zebras." She raised a finger and pointed across the field. "Go get 'em, yellow!" Abruptly, her hand fell into her lap. She closed her eyes and leaned against my shoulder.

Terry came walking back to the car.

"Is she still saying crazy stuff?" he asked.

"Purple polar bears," mumbled Jenny.

"Only if you count psychedelic *Wild Kingdom* as crazy," I replied.

"Well, we might as well get moving," said Cullison. He shut the door and moved around to take the driver's seat while Terry dropped into the passenger side. The sport utility wagon rumbled to life and headed back along the gravel road.

I leaned forward and spoke over the back of the seat. "Stop when you get to the accident."

"Why?" asked the mayor. "There's no one there."

"I've got a hunch there might be something there that we need."

A moment later Cullison brought the wagon to a halt beside the trio of wrecked vehicles. I climbed out. Ignoring the truck and the sedan, I went straight to Jenny Franklin's car and looked inside. It took me only a couple of seconds to find what I was looking for on the damp carpet of the passenger-side floorboards. I walked back to the station wagon and held out my hand to Cullison. "See if this doesn't come in handy."

The mayor's eyes brightened. "A cell phone. How did you know it was there?"

I shrugged. "Teenage girl, hundred-thousand-dollar car. A cell phone seems like a natural part of this equation." I shook the phone and rainwater dripped out. "I can't promise that it still works."

Cullison took the phone from my hand. He pulled the antenna and I heard the warming sound of a dial tone. "This is great," he said. He turned the phone off and shoved it into his pocket. "As soon as we get Jenny to the clinic, I'll get in touch with the state."

I climbed back in beside the delirious girl and Cullison headed for Meridian at high speed. At one point he steered the station wagon around a curve so fast that the tall four-by-four swayed precariously. I was beginning to wonder if we were going to be in an accident of our own when Cullison skidded to a halt in front of a low brick building. "This is the place."

The clinic was not very impressive looking, but at least it was new and appeared clean. Cullison and Terry held Jenny Franklin between them as they led her up the steps into the building while I followed behind. Inside, I was surprised to find the place a hive of activity. At least a dozen people were up and moving around. Twice that number were stretched out on tables, slumped in chairs, or lying under blankets on the tiled floor.

Seeing all the people made me feel like I was coming out of some strange postapocalyptic dream in which a handful of survivors wandered around a bombed-out world.

Dr. Benedict brought me back to reality when he emerged from a door at the end of the hallway and marched our way. He had slipped on a white medical jacket over his casual shirt and had a stethoscope hanging from his neck. Dressed as he was, he looked like a stock character from any medical show of the last twenty years. But the professional wear did nothing to impair the doctor's unique charm.

"I see you're done playing tourists," he said. It wasn't quite a sneer, but it was close.

This time even the easygoing Mayor Cullison seemed offended by the doctor's sharp tone. "We were inspecting the situation," he said, easing Jenny Franklin into a metal folding chair. "And we were looking for people."

"Well, while you were out inspecting and looking, people have been coming here for help," said Benedict.

Cullison nodded. "So I noticed."

"I believe you have emergency medical experience."

The mayor shook his head. "Only a couple of courses. I was going to be an EMT, but I dropped out."

Benedict gave his thin smile. "Well," he said, "here's your chance to see what you're missing." He pointed to an older couple huddled together in the corner of the front room. "The Hendersons have a variety of minor injuries. Nothing a little competent first aid can't handle."

Cullison looked ready to refuse, but after a moment he nodded. "I don't know how competent I'll be, but I'll give it a try."

As he walked across the room toward the waiting patients, the doctor turned his attention on me and Terry. "What about you two?" he asked. "Do you have any medical knowledge?"

To my surprise, Terry nodded. "I've had Red Cross training," he said. "And I'm a volunteer fireman."

"Good," said Benedict. "Go wash your hands and join me in the back. We have a young patient with a broken leg. I may need assistance."

Terry's face brightened. "Sure!" he said. "Right away." He went toward the back at a near run, leaving me to face the surly doctor on my own.

"And what about you?" he asked. "Any first-aid training?"

I shook my head. "I'm afraid not."

Benedict snorted. "Why am I not surprised?" He waved toward the door. "If you can't help, then the best thing you can do is stay out of the way."

That was a deal I was more than ready to accept. If we were going to be stuck in Meridian, I wanted a chance to prowl around on my own. "I'll go," I agreed. "But before I do, I have a couple of questions."

The doctor shook his head. "I don't have time to answer your silly questions. I have patients to attend to." He spun officiously on his heel and marched back down the hall.

I scowled at his back, then hurried after him. "It's about the apples," I called.

Benedict froze. "Apples?" he said without turning.

"Yes." I caught up to the doctor and moved around to stand in front of him. "Do you know Mrs. Myrtle?"

"I know almost everyone on this island," said Benedict.

"Good," I said. "Then you should know if Jean Myrtle was at the Apple Festival on Wednesday."

The doctor frowned. "I'm not certain. What does this have to do with anything?"

"Remember what Mayor Cullison said? His problems started at the Apple Festival." I crossed my arms and gave Benedict my best investigative-journalist stare. "What about you, Doctor. Where does your memory loss begin?"

"I'm not certain," said Benedict. He paused for a moment then shrugged. "It may have been around the time of the festival. If there is a disease being spread, we may all have contracted it there."

"Did you eat any apples at the festival?" I asked.

Benedict scowled. "Really, Ms. Skye. It was an apple festival. If you don't have anything more important to ask me—"

"Did you eat any apples?" I insisted.

"Yes," the doctor said with a disgusted sigh. "I ate several apples. So?"

"So, the pilot on the ferry was eating an apple, too. One that looked just like the apples I found at the fairgrounds."

The doctor took off his round glasses and polished them on the tail of his lab coat. Without the thick spectacles, his eyes were surprisingly large and intense. "You think the apples have something to do with the madness?"

I nodded. "I'm not certain, but what if there is no disease at all? What if it was something in the apples that caused everyone to go temporarily mad?"

There was a long silence before Benedict answered. "It's possible," he admitted, then put his glasses back on and looked at me. There was a new expression on his narrow face, one I couldn't quite interpret. If I didn't know better, I might have thought it was a look of respect. He mumbled something under his breath.

"What's that?" I asked.

"Nothing," said Benedict. "You may well be right about a substance in the food being responsible. That would fit the rapid pattern of development."

From another room there came a crash of metal followed by a muffled shout. A woman with tousled hair and a wrinkled dress popped out of a door and hurried up to Benedict's side. "Doctor, we're having trouble with the Heinemann girl," she said mournfully.

"She's hitting people, and we can't get her to stop. She's saying some of the most *terrible* things."

"Hang on one moment, Miss Shalansky," said the doctor. "I'll be right in." The woman nodded and retreated through the door. Benedict turned his attention back to me. "It may be that there is some advantage to having a reporter around after all, even if she works for a sleazy tabloid."

I stood up as straight as I could, looking the doctor right in the glasses. "I don't care what you think of my paper. I'm a good journalist."

"I hope so," said Benedict. "I sincerely do. Because I have an important task for you."

"What kind of task?"

"Believe it or not," said the doctor, "we have the same goal here. You want your story. I want to take care of my patients. But the first thing that both of us need is to understand what's happening on Meridian. To do that, you're going to need to take a little trip."

"I thought you said there was no way off the island."

"This trip is on the island," he said. "Do you have a car?"

I shook my head. "No. I mean, yes, I do have a car, but someone damaged it last night. It won't run."

The doctor took a ring of keys from the jacket of his lab coat and extended them toward me. "Here, take my car. It's the blue Olds on the corner."

I took the dangling keys from his hand. "Where am I supposed to go in your car?"

"Go north out of town, past the fairgrounds, and down the main highway till you come to a junction. Turn left and look for a field closed in by tall fences and wire." Having said this, Dr. Benedict turned away and started down the hall.

"Wait!" I shouted after him. "What am I looking for?"

"If you're half the journalist you think you are," he called over his shoulder, "you'll find that out for yourself."

I don't know when I had been so cheered by someone's confidence in my abilities.

NINE

I PROMISED TERRY NOT TO SPOT ANY MONSTERS WHILE HE wasn't looking. Not that any seemed to be around. For a disaster area, Meridian was beautiful.

Under the noon sun and the rain-scrubbed blue sky, the rolling hills of the little island were thick and brilliant green. Fall had only begun to touch the leaves of the orchards, adding a few freckles of yellow and brown. Only the impossibly orderly rows of trees and the occasional glint of a bright yellow apple revealed that the luxuriant forests on the hills were planned, not natural. Between the orchards, the valleys were lined with fields of brown corn and pastureland spotted with handfuls of off-white sheep.

Dr. Benedict's big Oldsmobile sedan drifted over the rutted road like an ocean liner cresting rolling waves. I rolled down the windows and let fresh, loam-scented air blow through the car. The weather was warming, on its way to hot. After the gloom and storms of the previous day, and the madness of the long night, it felt like morning had finally arrived.

I made two passes along the road before I finally spotted the turnoff that Benedict had described, and even then my first try brought me to a quick dead end. Eventually I settled on what I hoped was the right road. The course led west along a twisting, wayward path that curved up and down the back of a round-backed ridge. Twenty minutes later there was still no sign of the fence Benedict had mentioned and I was starting to wonder if I had taken a wrong turn after all. What *was* in view was the edge of the island. Beyond it the brown Mississippi was flecked with patches of roiling foam as it hustled over sandbars and around islets of mud.

I was on the verge of asking myself if the whole thing had been a snipe hunt designed to get me out of Dr. Benedict's hair when a glint of silver appeared over a field ahead. There was a fence after all. The orchard on the right side of the road ended abruptly and was replaced by a chain-link fence that enclosed a low field of green plants. As I got closer I saw that it wasn't just a fence, it was more like a fortress. There was a double wall of chain link separated by a dozen feet of bare ground strewn with loose coils of razor wire. More razor wire topped the fences, along with light posts at regular intervals.

My first thought was that the fence had to contain a maximum-security prison, but the fields on the other side were a thick patchwork of wheat at various stages of ripeness. At the far end of the formidable fence was a metal gate with a large lock and a small sign.

AGROTEX
EXPERIMENTAL FARM #12
NO TRESPASSING

Agrotex rang no bells for me, and I had little idea why Benedict had sent me to this place. But there was something about high fences and closed gates that always got me interested. Anything that was being hidden so well had to be worth checking out.

I pulled the doctor's car into the drive and strolled up to the gate. There was no bell, or buzzer, or any other way I could see to get the attention of anyone inside the fence. Standing on tiptoes, I could just make out a long, low-roofed building a dozen yards on the other side of the gate.

"Hey!" I shouted. "Anyone home?" There was no answer.

At that point the rules of journalism demanded that I either wait for someone to show up or go home. Even newspapers like the *Global Query,* which have morals as flexible as fresh taffy, don't generally condone breaking and entering on the part of their reporters— or, at the very least, they don't condone being caught at it.

But in this case I figured I was due an exception. After all, people all over Meridian were going bonkers. I wasn't going in there to get a story. I was going in there to check on whoever was inside in case they needed medical attention. It was a humanitarian gesture.

I won't pretend that I believed this, but I thought I could sell it to the jury.

Getting under the gate turned out to be a little harder than I expected. On a day when I had eaten nothing but a double handful of granola, and during which I had walked for miles, it seemed reasonable that I should be able to slide through a small opening. After all, it felt like my belly button and spinal cord were trying to kiss. However, one day's starvation had done nothing to reduce the girth of my derriere. Halfway through, I found myself wedged facedown, eating dust as I attempted to wiggle my rear under the bar.

"Uh, I don't think you're supposed to do that," said a deep voice from above.

I twisted my head around and saw a tall, square-jawed black man standing over me. He wore a pale blue lab coat over a charcoal polo shirt and jeans that were so crisp and deep blue I doubted they had ever seen the inside of a washing machine. His bright green eyes were startling next to his dark skin and black hair.

"I wanted to see if you were all right," I said.

"I'm fine," he said in a bass rumble.

"Good. That's good." I pushed myself forward with my toes and pulled against the gravel with my hands, giving a very unladylike grunt in the process, but I failed to extract myself from under the gate. I tilted my head back and looked up at the man in the lab coat. "Since you're so fine, would you help me get out of here?"

"I suppose I could." He crouched down at my side. "Would you prefer I pull or push?"

I did my best to shrug. "Pull. I'd hate to think I'd come this far for nothing."

He slid his hands under my shoulders and took a

grip on my shirt. "Please excuse the familiarity," he said.

"You're excused."

With a sharp tug, and a last painful attempt to compress my posterior, I popped under the gate and rolled free on the other side. The man helped me to my feet. "Are you all right?" he asked.

I brushed at the dirt and fragments of leaves on my clothing. "That seems to be the question of the day," I said. "Yes, I'm fine."

The black man stretched out his hand. "I'm Steven Kumal." Now that I was standing up, I could see that he was very tall, at least six-foot-five, even taller than Terry. Standing next to him, I felt like a six-year-old looking up at an adult.

"Savvy Skye," I said. I was surprised at how easily the pseudonym dropped from my tongue. This secret-identity business was getting easier. I reached out to shake his hand and his big fingers swallowed mine like a Doberman downing a Chihuahua. "Do you work for Agrotex?"

Kumal nodded. "Yes, I most certainly do." His voice was so deep and smooth, his manner so calm, it made me feel a little sleepy just to listen to him. "It's very nice to meet you, Ms. Skye," he continued. "But would you mind telling me why you were stuck under Agrotex's gate?"

"I wasn't stuck," I said. I brushed dirt from the protuberance that had blocked my passage. "Like I already said, I was coming in to see that you're all right."

Kumal thought this over for a moment, his expression impassive. He made a noise that might have been a sigh, but it was low enough to make my teeth rattle. "It seems to me that if you were willing to risk entering as you did, you must have had some reason to believe that I might be in danger."

I nodded. "With what's going on all over the rest of the island, it seemed like someone should check this place."

A frown marred Kumal's composure. "Is something wrong with the rest of the island?"

I pushed my tangled hair away from my face and stared into the man's green eyes. "You don't get out much, do you, Mr. Kumal."

"Actually," he replied, "it's Doctor Kumal."

"Is it?"

"Yes. I'm the director of this facility."

I smiled. "Congratulations, I'm sure."

He gave a slow nod. "Thank you. But you were correct in your assumption. It's been several days since I have left this compound."

"Take my word for it. Things are pretty strange out there. People are going nuts all over the island, buildings are burning down, the fairgrounds are a wreck, the ferry is missing, and—" I stopped and nodded toward the building. "You think maybe we could go inside and talk about it?"

Kumal shoved his hands into the pockets of his lab coat. "I'm not certain that we can. This is supposed to be a closed facility."

"Oh, really?" I asked, putting as much innocence into the question as I could manage. "Why is that?"

He folded his arms across his polo shirt. "I believe

that would be because Agrotex doesn't want anyone coming in here," he replied. His arms bulged with muscles that looked more suitable for a baseball player than a scientist.

It was a perfect nonanswer. I decided to change direction. "So, what do you do here?"

This time Kumal was a little slower to answer. "All right. Let's go inside," he said at last. "You can tell me what's wrong with the rest of Meridian."

"Great," I said with a smile. "I'd love to take a look around."

Kumal was silent as he led the way into the building. At the door I was met by a blast of heat and humidity that turned my hair into an instant mass of frizzies. Clouds of mist swirled around our feet as we stepped through a small gloomy entry hall and into a large room that was brilliantly lit by both skylights and an incredible array of blue-white grow lamps. Long tables ran the length of the narrow building. The tables were topped by thousands of tiny acrylic flowerpots, each of which held a small seedling of an almost painfully bright green under the intense light.

"What kind of plants are these?" I asked.

"QT-one-one-seven," said Kumal, walking along the side of the table with rapid strides.

I hurried to keep up. "What's that?"

"Wheat."

I picked up one of the pots in passing and looked at the tiny green stalk. It didn't look like much more than a blade of grass. "Why are you growing wheat?" I called after Kumal. "You guys run a bakery some- where?"

"You wouldn't want to bake anything with these plants," Kumal replied. "They're poisonous."

I dropped the little pot to the table. "You're growing poisonous wheat?"

"Oh, yes," he said. "In fact, I should warn you not to touch it."

"Now he tells me," I mumbled under my breath.

Kumal stopped in front of a table that was burdened with enough electrical gear to run the space shuttle. Despite the mass of metal and wires, the desk looked so neat you could eat off it—if you dared eat anything in a place that grew poisoned wheat. "One moment," said Kumal. "I need to check in with headquarters."

He sat down in front of the computer screen and hammered a quick succession of keys. Despite the enormous size of his hands, his long fingers moved across the keyboard quite nimbly. A window appeared in the corner of the computer monitor. It took me a moment to realize that the window showed a miniature view of another office, this one occupied by a woman in a rather severe dark suit.

"Steven," said a sharp voice from the computer's speaker. "We were about to contact you. There are rumors on the radio that something has gone wrong on Meridian."

"Yes, there does seem to be something going on outside," said Kumal.

The computer relayed the clear sound of disgust made by the woman at the other end of the connection. "Don't tell me. More protesters?"

The station director shook his head. "Not this time. From what I understand, there is a problem with the people on the island behaving in an irrational fashion. There has been some destruction."

"Do you know the cause?"

"I have not determined that as of yet." Kumal shifted around in his seat.

"Damn," said the woman on the monitor. "Do you think this is a wildfire situation? We can get a team—"

"I have a visitor here," Kumal said quickly. "Perhaps we should discuss this later."

The woman on the screen leaned in close, her face filling the window. "You let someone else inside the building?"

"Ms. Skye came here to warn me." The station director turned to me and waved me closer to the computer. "Would you mind coming over here and repeating what you told me?"

I took a cautious step toward the computer. Something was going on here, something I didn't quite understand, but I was beginning to suspect that Dr. Benedict had indeed had good reason for sending me to this place. "People have been going crazy," I said at last. "All over the island."

Kumal kept his extraordinary eyes focused on me. "How would you characterize this behavior?" he asked. "Are delusions or hallucinations involved?"

I thought of Mayor Cullison's marauding samurai and nodded. "You could say that."

"Paranoia? Violence?"

"Yeah. That, too. Do you know something about this?"

Kumal turned back to his screen. "Did you hear?"

"I heard." The woman closed her eyes and nodded.

"Do you feel that some type of . . . intervention will be required?"

"So it would seem."

"I thought you told me that was impossible," the woman said with more than a trace of bitterness.

Kumal gave another of his deep rumbling sighs. "It *is* impossible," he said. "But considering the circumstances, it might be prudent to get more personnel to the island as soon as possible."

"Yes," said the woman on the screen. "We . . ." She paused, and a teeny frown crossed her pint-sized image. "What did you say your visitor's name was?"

"Ms. Skye, Savvy Skye." Kumal glanced round at me again. "Why, is it important?"

"Savvy Skye," repeated the woman. "Skye . . ." She suddenly froze and stared hard into the camera. She raised her hand and pointed a Lilliputian finger my way. "I'll say it's important. I've seen her picture a hundred times. She's a reporter for the *Global Query*."

I groaned. Out of all the corporate bigwigs in the world, I had to run into one that slummed in the supermarket aisle.

Kumal turned back to me, that flat expression on his face unchanged. "A reporter," he repeated. "How interesting."

TEN

THE BIG MAN LIFTED A FOOT-LONG METAL SPIKE AND HELD IT UP to catch the light. "Now what am I to do with you?" he asked, his voice as calm as ever.

I bit my lip and shrugged nervously. "You could let me go," I suggested.

Kumal smiled. It was the first time I had seen any real expression on his dark face. "Do you actually think I would try and hold you here?"

"You mean . . . you're not?" From the way the computer woman had talked, I had almost expected to find myself being turned into fertilizer for their crop of deadly cereal.

The director shook his head and carefully put the spike down on the table at his side. "I'm not the police, Ms. Skye. Had you entered this property illegally, I might have some grounds to detain you. However, since I aided your entry, I don't believe there's any legal way I could hold you here against your will."

I eyed the gleaming point of the spike and nodded

toward the table. "What are you going to do with that?"

Kumal glanced at the spike, then lifted it and held it out toward me. "This is a hygrometer. It's used to measure the moisture content of soil."

I took the spike from his hand. Though it looked like a huge nail, it was light as a knitting needle and had a row of tiny LED lights along one side. My feelings of impending dissection began to fade. "Water levels?"

"Precisely. I'm not going to hold you prisoner, Ms. Skye. Neither do I intend to hurt you." He settled into a chair and folded his big hands in his lap. "I assume you came to Meridian to get a story."

"Yes," I admitted. "But things here aren't quite what I expected. And I really did mean to see if you were all right."

"I appreciate that." For a moment the black man was silent. He sat still in his chair, his green eyes shut in thought. "The way I see it, I have only two choices," he began, eyes still closed. "Either I send you away from this facility and leave you to write whatever you want, or I answer your questions now and make sure that your information is correct."

I couldn't have been more stunned if he had threatened to poison me. Finding a company that actually volunteered to talk to the *Query* was an event that made the capture of a UFO seem commonplace. Such openness threw me completely out of my game. "That's a very rare attitude, Dr. Kumal. Most people will do whatever they can to hide from the press— especially from the *Query*."

The director opened his green eyes and nodded.

"I'm sure they do, but we have nothing to hide here."

That answer was just familiar enough to put me back on track. Nobody ever had anything to hide . . . until you asked the right questions.

I leaned back in my chair and gave Dr. Kumal my best investigative-journalist stare. "That brings up a good point, Mr. Director. Just what are you doing growing deadly poisonous plants?"

The big man got up from his chair and walked slowly around the end of the table. "We're not."

"But you said—"

He cut me off with a raised hand. "I said the plant you held was poisonous, but I said nothing about deadly." Kumal lifted one of the pots from the table. It looked like a thimble in his big hand. "See this number?" he asked, tapping his index finger against the side of the pot. "That indicates this plant is infected with *Hemifestus garlum*—red rust. It's a fungal infection that strikes both wheat and rye."

There was nothing wrong with the plant that I could see. "This red rust, is it poisonous?"

"It has a deleterious effect on the taste of wheat, but it's not truly toxic." Kumal returned the pot to the table and took up another. One glance at the label and he produced another of his peculiar deep rumbles. "Now this plant is carrying *Kalliti pallidus,* also known as snowcap. If you were to consume this plant, you might face some highly unpleasant digestive difficulties."

"But not death?"

The director shook his head. "There are over ten thousand seedlings here, and three acres of plants outside. Between them they carry some one hundred and twenty-four diseases. However, none of these diseases is deadly to humans." He returned the snowcap-afflicted plant to the table. "Statistically speaking, you'd be far more likely to die from an allergy to wheat itself than from any of the infections these plants carry."

I looked down the tables burdened with tiny plants and colorful diseases. "What's the point of all this?" I asked. "Are these diseases rare?"

"All too common," Dr. Kumal replied. He put his hands behind his back, laced his long fingers together, and resumed his slow trip around the table. "It's not the diseases which are unusual, it's the wheat."

"And what's so strange about wheat?"

The director kept walking, his face turned away from me. "Do you know anything about genetic engineering, Ms. Skye?"

The dusty old news-wire machines in the offices of the *Green River Journal* rang four bells for a major news story. The term *genetic engineering* sounded at least five loud clangs in my skull. Those words might as well have been boilerplate for half the stories we ran in the *Query*. Genetic engineering was a perfect modern bogeyman. No one really understood what it was, no one could define its limits, and even the scientists seemed nervous about what it might possibly cause.

"You mean these plants are mutants?" I asked. Headlines began to form in my mind: GENETIC ENGINEERING BREEDS KILLER GRAIN. MONSTER PLANTS OF THE MISSISSIPPI.

"They're not mutants," said Kumal. There was a

note of indignation in his voice. "Mutation is a random change. These plants have been very carefully created."

"To do what?"

"To resist infections of all sorts." Kumal spread his long arms in a gesture that took in the length of the warm bright room. "The diseases introduced to these plants would destroy most wheat plants before they matured. Outside, we have a field of plants which yields seventy percent of normal production despite having been exposed to molds and fungus. We have reason to believe that the plants you see in front of you will fight off all known infections."

"A kind of super wheat," I said.

This name seemed to please Dr. Kumal. He flashed another brief smile, his teeth bright against his dark skin. "Yes, super wheat. Wheat that can increase worldwide production by enough to feed tens of millions."

I nodded. "And put a few billion in the pocket of Agrotex?"

The director's smile vanished instantly. "We're not a charitable organization, Ms. Skye. No law says that we can't make an advancement in food production and a profit at the same time."

"You're right," I agreed. "There's nothing wrong with that." I studied Kumal's dark features. He didn't appear to be angry, but there was definitely a more aggressive set to his square jaw. It was time to open up with the big guns.

I dropped the hygrometer, stood up, and looked around the brightly lit room. Through a narrow win-

dow in the concrete-block wall I could see the gleaming coils of razor wire on the fences outside. "You
keep a lot of security around this place for someone
that has nothing to hide."

"The security provisions are there to protect the
casual visitor from harm," said Kumal. "Contact with
the plants could have unpleasant side effects. We have
had considerable . . . shall we say, difficulties in the
past, which required the establishment of strict measures."

"To keep out protesters?"

Kumal shook his head. "Not just protesters." He
gestured toward the door. "Come outside and I'll show
you why the fences are there."

I had a momentary qualm at the thought of ending
up buried in the silty ground, but I shook off my fears,
nodded, and followed him through the long, steamy
room and out into the morning sunshine. Compared
with the tropical heat and humidity inside, the warm
Indian-summer day along the Mississippi was almost
chilly.

Dr. Kumal led the way along a neatly edged gravel
path between twin fields choked with knee-high wheat.
The plants didn't seem to be unusual, and they didn't
seem to be covered with any kind of nasty disease. But
then, I was no expert on wheat. The only kind I had
seen before came shredded and ready to be dunked in
milk.

"What are we looking for?" I asked.

"This," said Kumal. He pointed to a spot near the
fence.

I walked closer and saw a trio of brown patches in

the field ahead. In each of them a circle of earth about four feet in diameter had been turned over, leaving dead stalks of brown wheat strewn across the ground and a hole filled with muddy water. "What happened here?"

Kumal pointed to a ragged tear in the fence that had been repaired with gleaming wire. "Someone cut their way in here and dug up our fields."

"Protesters?"

He nodded. "Let's say . . . intruders. We've had difficulty ever since we acquired the land for this facility two years ago. We've had over a dozen incidents of break-ins over the last six months." He ran his fingers over the metal suture in the chain-link fence. "As you can see, even our latest measures haven't completely stopped the break-ins."

I crouched down next to one of the brown circles. It was better than a foot deep, far more than was needed to destroy the wheat. At the bottom of the circle something metallic shone through a soupy mix of mud and water. "What is that down there?"

"It's part of our sprinkler system," said Kumal. "When rain is sparse, we supplement with sprinklers. We can't risk the experiment being interrupted by dry weather."

I backed up and stepped away from the brown patch, dark mud sticking to the soles of my shoes. "Do they always dig up your sprinkler system?"

"That's been the pattern." The director looked out at the orchards beyond the perimeter of the fence. "Unless this stops soon, we may be forced to electrify the fences."

"You're going to electrify the fences . . . to protect casual visitors?"

Kumal did not answer. Instead he turned and started walking back toward the building.

I hurried to keep up. "Tell me," I said, "what's the connection between what you're doing here and what's happening on the rest of the island?"

"I don't really know what's happening on the rest of the island," said Kumal, without breaking stride.

"I told you—madness, hallucinations, destruction." I paused a moment for dramatic effect, then added, "And death."

The director stopped in his tracks. "Death?"

"A murder," I said. "Apparently caused by the madness." I folded my arms and shrugged. "At least one. Maybe more."

Kumal pulled his big hands from behind his back and rubbed them together. I could hear the sound his dry palms made—it was like sandpaper in the quiet field. "We couldn't have had anything to do with that," he said. "It's not possible."

"It isn't?" I looked off at the shadowed spaces of the orchards and the rolling hills at the center of the island. "Tell me, Doctor, what does *wildfire* mean?"

The big man was slow to answer. "Wildfire?"

"That's what the woman on the computer said."

The director made another deep grumble. This time I imagined that it was less thoughtful and more like the rolling cough of an angry lion. "Wildfire is nothing but a contingency plan," he said.

"Contingency against what?"

There was an even longer pause. Finally Kumal

shook his head sharply. "Agrotex has absolutely nothing to do with whatever may have occurred elsewhere on the island. We use very strict procedures here." He cleared his throat and then waved toward the gate. "I'm afraid I have a lot of work to do, Ms. Skye. I'm going to have to ask you to leave."

Nothing lasts forever, I suppose, but actually having someone cooperate on a story had been nice while it lasted. I held out my hand toward Kumal. "Thank you, Doctor. Your information should be very helpful for my story."

The director stepped closer and shook my hand, but the calm that had dominated his expression earlier was gone. He pressed his lips into a hard line as he looked at me. "Agrotex has exceeded all standard safety precautions at this facility."

"Of course."

"And we have nothing to do with any deaths."

"Certainly not."

I followed him down the gravel path back to the gate. "Do I have to crawl under again?" I asked.

Kumal stepped forward quickly, pressed a button, and the gate swung open with a soft electric hum. "I want to thank you for coming out here," he said.

"No problem," I answered. "I enjoyed the visit." Which was the absolute truth.

Driving Benedict's whale of a car back to town, I thought over the information I had learned from Kumal and from the nameless woman on the computer screen. Before I had only had an island full of madmen and a little senseless violence to make sense of. Now I had added genetically engineered plants, protesters, break-ins, something called wildfire, and one hundred and twenty-four kinds of mold and fungus.

Suddenly I was very glad I had let Mr. Genovese bully me into coming to Meridian.

ELEVEN

I HAD BEEN AWAY FROM THE TOWN OF MERIDIAN NO MORE THAN two hours, but when I returned I found that the clinic had been invaded by astronauts.

No sooner did I come through the front door than an amplified voice shouted in my ears. "Halt! Stay where you are."

It was a needless warning. Considering the strangeness of the scene inside, there was little chance that I would do anything but stand there and gawk. The large front room of the clinic had been divided by sheets of translucent plastic, which were held to both floor and ceiling by what had to be a hundred yards of silver duct tape. Ultraviolet lights gleamed overhead, filling the room with a purplish glow and making everything white gleam like tiny neon tubes. The whole place smelled like the inside of a jug of bleach.

In the center of this impromptu entrance hall was a flimsy folding table covered in stacks of clipboards and a box of little goofy golf pencils. Strangest of all was the figure in a plump white suit and bucket-shaped helmet that was seated behind the table.

"Who are you?" I asked.

The space-suited figure stood up and shuffled toward me. Through the clear plate at the front of the helmet, I saw the face of a young woman with sharp, pretty features. She had honey-blond hair pulled tight in a bun and covered over with a hair net. The total effect was to make her look something like a futuristic fry cook.

"Do you know your name?" asked the woman. Her voice was distorted by the helmet, adding to the extraterrestrial drive-in experience.

"I know my name," I said. "How about you?" I took a step forward.

Immediately the woman raised something small and dark in her gloved right hand. "Give me your name," she demanded.

My first thought was that the device was some kind of high-tech thermometer. But as it came closer to my face I saw that it was some kind of stun gun. The arc of blue-white electricity that curved between the prongs of the little weapon looked tough enough to curl my eyebrows.

I swallowed hard and stepped back, my hands raised in what I hoped was the universal gesture for surrender. "What's going on here?"

"Your name!" said the woman in the suit. "What's your name?" There was a quaver in her voice that I recognized: she was terrified.

"Savannah McKinnon," I said quickly. "My name is Savannah McKinnon."

The woman seemed to relax a little. "Do you know where you are?"

I nodded. "I'm at the medical clinic in Meridian, Illinois. I'm tired and hungry and dirty and I've been up all night." I lowered my hands slowly. "But I'm not crazy and I'm not violent, and I would really, really appreciate it if you didn't shock me."

The electricity disappeared from the end of the weapon and the woman let her arm drop. "Sorry," she said. "We've been having some problems."

"Yeah, I imagine you have." I gave her a nice sane-person smile. "I've given you my name. Now, would you mind telling me who you are?"

"Kirin Havers," she replied. "Centers for Disease Control, Midwestern Emergency Operation."

"Who called you guys?"

"We received a call from the mayor of Meridian informing us of an emergency situation." The woman's posture inside her suit grew straighter. "The first CDC personnel were on the ground within thirty-five minutes."

There was an evident note of pride in her voice as she reported this information, and I had to admit I was impressed. I hadn't seen Mayor Cullison make any calls, but evidently he had put the car phone to good use. "So, have you guys had time to figure out what's going on around here?"

The woman shook her head, the plastic helmet crimping slightly as she turned. "So far we have over one hundred cases of aggravated dementia. Another sixty residents have reported experiencing symptoms. Approximately forty are currently unaccounted for."

Behind the translucent sheets of plastic I saw the blurry white forms of more people approaching. "What are you going to do with me now?"

"That depends," said Havers. "When did you recover from your delusional state?"

I shrugged. "As far as I know, I was never in any delusional state. No more than usual, anyway."

The CDC worker's eyes widened. "You haven't had any symptoms?"

"Nope," I said with a shake of my head.

There was a faint hiss of escaping air as a seam opened in the plastic sheet at the back of the room. Two more figures forced their way through the opening and waddled my way in their puffy coveralls. "You say you've experienced no hallucinations?" asked a man in one of the suits. He had a painfully short gray crew cut and eyes that were bombardier blue.

"None."

"No blackouts or periods of lost time?" asked the Asian woman in the other suit.

I shook my head. "Not that, either."

The three suited people turned toward each other, bending their heads together until their helmets almost touched. "We've only had one unaffected subject so far," whispered the man, "and his time of exposure was short. This woman could be the key."

"Do you think she's been exposed?" asked Havers. "We don't know anything of her history."

"With the kind of distribution we've been getting," said the other woman, "everyone on the island must have been exposed." She glanced at me for a moment, then turned back to the others. Her voice lowered to a barely audible whisper, but I could still make out phrases like *unmatched opportunity* and *immunity factor.*

I edged toward the door. From the way this little trio of medical witches was talking, I could foresee a long series of blood samples, throat cultures, observation, toil, and trouble in my future. That was definitely not in my plans. If I wanted to keep after this story, I was either going to have to run fast or do some equally quick thinking.

The little conference broke up before I worked up the energy to make a break for it. Kirin Havers left the others and picked up a clipboard from the table then walked back over to me. "You said your name is McKinnon?"

"Yeah."

Through the faceplate I saw her lips pucker in a frown. "I don't have a McKinnon on the list."

The man with the buzz cut rustled over to her side. "She has to be on the list. Everyone on the island is on the list."

"See for yourself."

Havers handed over the list to the man. He flipped quickly through the pages then looked at me. "How long have you been on the island, Ms. McKinnon?"

In general, I believe telling the truth is the best policy. But that doesn't mean there aren't times when the delivery of that truth shouldn't be a carefully considered business. I took a few seconds to consider my options. If I told the CDC that I had been on the island overnight, they might think I was their miracle key to a cure, which seemed to be a direct road to life as a pincushion. Needles are not my friend.

"I haven't been here long," I said at last. "I'm not a resident. I'm a reporter."

"Reporter?" The man flipped back through the pages. "We have a reporter listed as being on the island. A woman named Skye."

"My name's McKinnon," I replied. For once, I was very glad of Editor Bill Genovese and his penchant for pen names. I fished into my purse and produced my billfold. I flipped it open to my driver's license and held it up to his helmet. "See, McKinnon. M-C-K—"

The man pushed my billfold away. "How did you get here, Ms. McKinnon?"

I shrugged with studied casualness. "I heard there was trouble out here and hired a boat to bring me to the island."

The man looked around at the others. "It appears we don't have an immune response. We have a limited time of exposure."

"Exposure to what?" I said.

The man scowled at me. "You've walked into a potentially dangerous situation here, Ms. McKinnon. Didn't you know this island is under CDC quarantine?"

"No," I said honestly. I fought back a smile. If I played my cards right, it looked like I just might avoid the life of a lab rat, and wouldn't have to tell an outright lie to do so. A little creative recounting of the facts had considerably reduced my value as a source of plasma. I dug through my purse again and pulled out my tape recorder.

"Why is the island under quarantine?" I asked.

The man looked at the recorder like it was a slab of spoiled liver with a side order of rotten onions. "We don't have time for the press right now," he snarled. "We're in the middle of a medical crisis."

He leaned in close to me. I had the impression that if I had been a man, I would have been on the receiving end of a good finger jab to the chest. "I'm going to say this one time," he snapped, "so listen closely. This island is under strict quarantine. From this moment on, you are to be treated as if you have been exposed to an infectious agent." He paused. Small drops of spittle ran down the inside of his faceplate in the aftermath of his lecture. "Do you understand me?"

"Yes," I said. "But I am a reporter. I'm used to danger." I tried to make it sound breezy—Savannah McKinnon, ready to brave the bullets to get her story. Crew Cut was not impressed.

"Stow it," he said curtly. "You are not to leave this island without the permission of CDC, neither are you to bring anyone else here. I won't risk spreading this infection any further. Is that clear, Ms. McKinnon?"

"Sure." I held my recorder close to the man's helmet. "But just what *is* going on here?" I asked. "An epidemic? Has Ebola entered the heart of America?"

Old Blue Eyes gave me another good glare, then spun around. "Ms. Havers, take this person and give her a five-minute tour. Five minutes. No longer. Answer her questions and get her out of the way."

"Yes, sir," said Havers. "Then what?"

"Then she's on her own. She's to be allowed in any

area but the clean room. If she wants to expose herself, that's her own business. If she gives you any trouble . . . just let me know." I had the distinct impression that he would have been pleased to see me come down with something nice and deadly should I prove to be less than totally compliant.

"Yes, sir," Havers repeated.

The buzz cut and his associate retreated through the back door without another word and faded away behind the plastic walls. Kirin Havers turned to me when they were gone. From her expression, it was clear that playing tour guide was not among her favorite duties.

"What do you want to see?" she asked with a sigh.

I pretended to consult my notes. "What can you tell me about this epidemic, Ms. Havers? Have you identified the agent?"

"Kirin."

"What's that?"

She shrugged, causing her suit to rustle. "You might as well call me Kirin," she said. "And we haven't identified an agent, but we're working on it." She held out a gloved hand.

I shook it—her grip felt odd and stiff through the suit. "Nice to meet you. Do you do this kind of thing often?"

"Never," said Kirin. "I mean, I've worked for CDC for years, but this is the first time we've ever had a real epidemic to deal with."

"How does that make you feel?"

She looked around, then leaned in close to me and whispered, "I'm scared out of my mind."

"Good for you," I replied. "It'll probably keep you alive."

Kirin smiled nervously. "I hope so."

I returned her smile. "So, Kirin, what's going on around this loony bin? Do they think it's an actual disease?"

"We don't know," she admitted. "Right now we're treating it like it's some kind of disease, but the truth is we don't know." She frowned. "We're doing about five thousand tests on everything from the water to the soil to the air, but we won't have the results back for several hours. Sorry."

"That's okay." I made another purse-diving expedition, rummaged past some empty gum wrappers, pulled out an old laundry ticket, and pretended to read something from its stained surface. "I'd like to talk to this local doctor. . . . I believe his name is Benedict?"

"Dr. Benedict has been exposed to the agent," she informed me. "We're allowing him to treat minor injuries, but he is currently in level-two quarantine."

"Can I go in there?"

"I don't see why not, since you've already been exposed. Follow me."

Kirin pushed through the plastic wall. I followed behind her. Though I knew I was being subjected to nothing more noxious than what I had already experienced on my first trip through the clinic, there was something about the maze of plastic walls and the workers in their space suits that made it all seem much more serious. The fact that I was not wearing one of the germ-repellent suits made me feel something like

I did in my recurring dreams about high school—the ones where I found myself sitting in Mrs. Tichen's homeroom in nothing but my underwear.

Behind the walls of plastic sheeting and duct tape, the patients of the Meridian Clinic were being administered treatment. I spotted a couple of children being cared for by a CDC worker in his heavy suit. Across the room my would-be werewolf was receiving attention from a man dressed in surgical scrubs. From the heavy purple-and-blue bruises on wolf guy's forehead, it was obvious that his delusions of monsterhood had not protected him from physical harm.

I was almost past the table when I finally realized the identity of the person who was treating the man's injuries. "Terry?"

Terry looked up and grinned at me. There were a series of stains on his shirt that appeared to be made by substances generally better left on the inside of human bodies. The thought that my mentally challenged colleague had been acting in any sort of medical capacity made me exceedingly glad that I still counted myself among the ranks of the healthy.

"Hey, Savvy," he called with a wave of a gloved hand "Did you find anything?"

"Do you know this man?" asked Kirin. "I thought you just got here."

"We sort of met before," I said. "Excuse me a moment. I need to go talk with him." I hurried over to Terry's side.

"I was afraid you wouldn't—" he started.

I clamped a hand over his mouth. "Quiet," I whispered to him. "Don't say anything about knowing me, or about me being in Meridian before. Understand?"

"Sure," he replied, his voice muffled by my hand. "I guess."

I took away my hand and looked around. Kirin was staring at us oddly, but at least she didn't seem ready to charge off and summon her superior. I wasn't sure if my story about having just arrived had really been necessary, or if Kirin would turn me in if she found out the truth, but it didn't seem like a good idea to carry out the experiment of finding out.

"Did you find anything out there?" Terry asked, matching my whisper.

I considered my answer for a moment. The trip had brought me a lot of interesting information, but on the Terry scale of weirdness, it wasn't particularly exciting. After all, there were no hairy apes, aliens, or vampires in sight. "I think I might have some leads on what's going on," I told him. "Can you get away long enough to take some pictures?"

Terry frowned. "I'm not sure. Since they found out that I didn't go crazy, they've been taking blood samples from me about every ten minutes." He tilted his head and looked at me. "They probably want samples from you, too."

Suddenly my little white lie seemed like a very good idea. "Not yet," I replied.

"At least they've been letting me help out with the people that are hurt," said Terry, "but they wouldn't let me go look for you." He glanced toward the back of the clinic, where a cluster of CDC personnel were bent over a heap of gleaming equipment. "I should probably tell them I found the person I was looking for. I wouldn't want them to be worried."

"No, no," I said quickly. I didn't want to do anything that would cause the CDC to reevaluate my situation. I reached out and patted one of the few unstained patches on Terry's arm. "It looks like you're really needed here. Why don't you stay and help? We can get the pictures I want when you're done."

He looked a little confused. "You're sure?"

"Absolutely." I looked around the room. "I'll go check things out. You just keep doing what you've been doing."

"Hey," the man on the table suddenly said. "Aren't you supposed to be working on my head?"

"Sure," Terry replied. "Just a second." Indecision tightened his features. "Are you sure I should stay? Maybe they'd let me go if you asked."

"There's a quarantine in effect on the island," I reminded him. "Nobody comes on, nobody gets off. We'll have plenty of time on Meridian to get pictures before other papers and TV stations start to show up."

Relief brightened Terry's face and I got a momentary glimpse of dimples. "Okay," he said. "See you later."

"Do you know him?" Kirin asked again as I rejoined her.

"He used to work with me," I replied. My string of half-truths was starting to get long.

She looked past me and watched Terry as he worked. My first thought was that she had put the McKinnon–Skye picture together and was about to call for the marines, but it soon became clear that Kirin

Havers's thoughts were traveling along a different highway. "So you two aren't, you know, dating or anything?" she asked.

I turned my head to look at Terry. He was cute. In his surgical scrubs, he could have been an extra from some medical show. *Young Dr. Handsome.* "No," I said. "Terry and I never dated. In fact, I don't think he's dating anyone right now."

"Really . . ." Kirin responded in a slow, considering voice. There was no doubt she was going to end Terry's datelessness if she could.

"We're supposed to be going to see Dr. Benedict," I reminded her.

Reluctantly, Kirin turned away from Terry and led me deeper into the clinic. We bypassed the crowd of workers at the back of the main room and slipped through another door in the plastic walls. Inside I saw several of the people that had been in the clinic on my first visit. Most of their wounds appeared to be minor, but in one sealed-off corner of the room Dr. Benedict stood over a figure sprawled on an examining table. Even from a distance I could see that the isolated patient was Jenny Franklin.

I started toward the doctor, but Kirin grabbed my arm. "I better get back to the door," she said. "Five minutes are up."

"That's all right," I told her with a smile. "I can take it from here."

Dr. Benedict looked up as I approached. "So," he said, "the great investigator returns." There was enough acid in his voice to strip the paint off a battleship.

I ignored his gibe for the moment as I looked down at Jenny. It was hard to believe this was the same girl we had found at the fairgrounds. Then, she had been confused, bruised, and muddy, but she had still appeared healthy. Now her skin had gone an unhealthy yellow. The muscles of her face appeared slack, and there was a puffy, swollen look to her limbs.

"What's wrong with her?" I asked, feeling a fresh surge of fear. "Is this part of the disease? Is it going to happen to everyone?"

"No," replied the doctor. He reached to the girl's wrist and fingered a silver bracelet that I hadn't noticed before. "Ms. Franklin is a diabetic," he said as he flipped over a charm bearing a tiny red cross. "She may not have had an insulin injection for several days. Her body's organs have suffered considerable damage."

I thought about the Mercedes convertible Jenny had been driving. It was obvious that she was rich, but money had not prevented her from having one truly terrible day. "Is she going to be okay?" I asked.

The doctor reached out and took hold of Jenny's wrist. "It's too early to tell. With the quarantine in place, I can't fly her out for treatment. I've ordered some tests. We can only hope they come back in time." He dropped her limp hand and looked at me, his eyes bright behind his thick glasses. "So tell me, did you make your way out to the experimental farm?"

I nodded. "I found it, all right. But I still don't understand what it has to do with the disease."

Benedict put his hands to his hips and scowled at

me. "You mean you went out there and learned nothing?"

I scowled right back. I was too tired and too hungry to take much more abuse. "I learned plenty. I found out about the genetically engineered plants, and the protesters, and Agrotex's security plans. All I don't know is what makes you think there's a connection between the farm and all the craziness on the rest of the island."

For a moment the doctor was silent. Then he shook his head slowly. "I can't believe it."

"What?"

"You missed the most important thing!" he shouted. "The problem isn't with the wheat, it's with the *fungus*."

I felt a wave of confusion strong enough to make my head swim. "How can the fungus be the problem? It's the wheat that's genetically engineered."

Dr. Benedict growled something under his breath. I couldn't understand a word, and from his tone I wasn't sure I wanted to. "Come with me," he demanded, once he was done cursing. "I'll show you."

We left Jenny Franklin lying on the table and went into a small office. From the bright orange boxes crammed into every corner, it was clear the CDC personnel had put the space to use as a storage area, but one small desk had been cleared to make room for a microscope and the wrinkled remains of a yellow apple.

"There," said Benedict with a gesture toward the scope. "Take a look."

I held my hair back with one hand and leaned over the scope. As usual, my first sight was darkness, followed by a detailed view of my own eyelashes. Finally I managed to position my eye properly and catch a high-resolution view of rotten fruit. Under the bright illumination of the scope I saw a landscape of waxy gold, spotted with light brown freckles and a scattering of something that looked like coffee grounds.

"What am I supposed to be looking at?" I asked.

"You're looking at the cause of the disturbances in Meridian," said Dr. Benedict. "Those dark spots are *Claviceps purpurea*."

I took my eye away from the microscope and looked up at him. "Should I know what that is?"

Benedict snorted. "I wouldn't expect you to know." He reached past me and snapped off the light on the microscope. "This is information that requires something of an education."

"Can you tell me now and gloat later?" I asked as politely as I could.

"Let's start with the basics. *C. purpurea* is a mushroom," he informed me, then paused and looked at me with a raised eyebrow. "Perhaps you've seen one of those?"

"Every time I have a pizza," I answered. I picked up the fragment of apple from the tray of the microscope and squinted at the yellow skin. The dark grains I had seen under the scope were barely visible as tiny pinpricks of black on the glossy skin. "Are you telling me this whole town is stoned on magic mushrooms?"

Benedict shook his head. "No. It's not that at all. Psylocybin mushrooms are only marginally dangerous." He took the apple from my hand, looked at it for a moment, then threw it into a trash can across the room. "What's going on in Meridian is more serious. A lot more serious." He stared at me hard. "In fact, there's a good chance that Meridian could be the starting place for the greatest plague since the Black Death."

TWELVE

KILLER MUSHROOMS OF MERIDIAN. IT WAS A PERFECT *QUERY* headline, and Mr. Genovese would love it. The only trouble was that I could make no sense out of it.

"How can mushrooms be such a great threat to Western civilization?" I asked.

Dr. Benedict pushed aside one of the stacks of supplies and reached behind it. He came out with a dusty book in a leather cover that was worn down slick. Without a word, he flipped through pages until he came to an illustration. Then he turned the book around and shoved it at me. "Take a look at this."

I took the book from his hands and drew it up in front of my face for a better look. The image on the page was a reproduction of an old woodcut. It showed a scene of chaos, with flames lapping at the sides of houses and bodies sprawled across the ground. Snarling dogs tore at the dead while clouds of black crows whirled overhead. Amid all the destruction, dozens of people stood frozen in what seemed to be some frenzied dance. Below the scene was a simple caption: *St. Anthony's Fire.*

"What is this?" I asked. I flipped the page and found another woodcut image. This time it was a man down on all fours, with foam running from his mouth. Mad eyes glared out of the drawing.

"It's usually called ergot," said Benedict. "It's the way this particular mushroom survives the winter. It forms a hard sclerotium."

Ergot rang faint bells somewhere back in my skull, but this was one story that was definitely going to require the use of a dictionary. "I thought ergot was a drug."

The doctor nodded. "It's the root source for dozens of drugs. Some of them even you may have heard of, like LSD."

"LSD?" If Benedict was telling the truth, the idea certainly made sense. Everyone in Meridian hadn't really gone mad, they were just off on a town-wide magical mystery tour. I looked back at the pictures in the book. "I take it something like this has happened before."

"Hundreds of times. Ergot has killed more people than Ebola and AIDS combined."

"Then why have I never heard Dan Rather talk about it?"

"Because," said Benedict, "there hasn't been an outbreak of ergot in over a hundred years." He pulled the book from my hands and slammed it shut, sending up a cloud of dust. "People learned to keep grain in dry storage, and the incidence of the fungus was drastically reduced."

"Grain?" I reached for the book. "Does it say anything in there about apples?"

"No." Benedict turned around and shoved the book back into its space between the boxes. "Ergot is known only as a parasite of rye, wheat, and other cereal grains. It also happens to be one of the diseases that Agrotex is experimenting with on their wheat."

I nodded. "All right, now I understand why you sent me out to the farm. But how did this ergot get from the wheat to the apples?"

"That's what makes this case so extraordinary." The doctor leaned toward me, his eyes shining with an excitement that leaked past his thick glasses. "We're witnessing something very special here—a transpecific migration of a parasite."

My first thought was that this was a phrase Terry would love. Mr. Genovese would have been another admirer. Ordinarily, I love a good scientific theory, myself, especially when it's filled with scary phrases I can use to pad out a story. But between Latinate mushrooms, *Über*-wheat, and species-hopping parasites, I was approaching my limits. "You're telling me that this mushroom, which has lived on grass for the last thousand years, has decided to go on a fruit diet?"

Benedict frowned. "I suppose it would be too much to expect that you would understand." He lifted his hand and shook a finger in my face. "This is a tremendous threat. Should this infection escape the island, it could spread to orchards all over the country. All over the world!"

For a moment I had a vision of men in dark shades peddling apples on shadowed street corners. Homeless apple addicts. Appleholics Anonymous. I put a hand over my mouth and stifled a laugh.

Benedict blinked in surprise. "You think there's something funny in this situation?"

I shook my head. "Mostly I think I'm way, way too tired for any of this." I got myself under control and drew in a deep breath. "Look, Doc, I'm willing to buy your fearsome fungus theory."

"It's not a theory."

"Whatever." I leaned back against a stack of crates filled with whatever it was the CDC thought was appropriate for a Midwestern epidemic. "Like I was saying, I'll buy that ergot is the cause for what's going on here. It fits the evidence, and besides, it makes a good story. But what I don't believe is that this stuff suddenly decided to take a vacation at the local orchard."

Benedict folded his arms and tilted his chin in the air. "Then how do you explain the presence of the fungus on the apples recovered from the fairgrounds?"

I paused before speaking, and looked the doctor in the eye. "I have a theory."

The doctor gave a laugh of his own. "*You* have a theory?"

"Yep." I pushed back my hopelessly tangled hair and smiled. "My theory is that someone put it there."

Benedict's eyes went so wide that his glasses were rimmed in white. "Who could . . . how . . ."

I reached out and patted him on the arm. "Don't worry, Doc. Journalists are trained to think the worst of people. Now, what do you know about the protesters at Agrotex?"

The doctor seemed only a step away from apoplexy, but he managed to choke down a breath. "The protesters?"

I nodded. "The director of the farm said they'd had trouble with people protesting the existence of the farm."

"Yes," said Benedict. "I do know something about that." He paused for a second, and seemed to recover from my suggestion of foul play. "Getting permission to field-test a genetically engineered plant drew quite a bit of attention. At one time or another we've had everyone from Greenpeace to the Audubon Society out here."

"Any of them stick around?"

The doctor nodded. "Meridian Is Our Home."

"I take it that's the name of an organization?"

"It's a group of people that want to keep Meridian from changing," said Benedict. "They protested the farm, and stopped the bridge project."

From glimpses of green hills and unspoiled countryside I had seen that afternoon, I could understand why someone would want to keep Meridian from being overrun by the ten-billionth set of golden arches. But there is no terrorist so adamant as a patriot, and no patriot so dangerous as one with high ideals. "Do you know any of the people that are involved in this Meridian Is Our Home group?"

"You've already met one," replied the doctor. "Mayor Cullison is one of the group's leaders."

That was certainly interesting information. "And where is your esteemed mayor?"

Benedict shook his head. "I don't know. He placed

the call to the CDC, and then he left. I haven't seen him since then."

My spider senses began to tingle. "Who else is in this group?"

"Let me see. . . ." Benedict rubbed his round chin for a moment, then snapped his fingers. "There's Corrie Crocker, she's been part of MIOH from the beginning."

"And do you know where I can find Ms. Crocker?"

Five minutes later I was back in Benedict's blue Olds, rolling toward the north side of the island. For someone that had been up almost continuously for two days, and who hadn't eaten a bite in almost as long, I was feeling pretty good. Finally, the insanity on Meridian was starting to make some sense.

At the end of a long gravel road I came to a colorful sign.

APPLE FRUIT PACKING CO.
ALL FRUIT 100% ORGANIC
C. Crocker, Proprietor

In my experience, organic fruit was another name for puny, bug-eaten apples and bananas that were just one step away from becoming brown Jell-O. But from what I could see of the trees on the Crocker farm, this was one place where organic and inedible did not overlap. The limbs of the apple trees were so burdened with fruit that they leaned down around the road like a green tunnel.

The road turned into a drive, and the drive into a roughly circular parking lot occupied by a decrepit tractor and an equally ancient VW Bug. There was a large rambling house shaded by a pair of giant oaks and a small fruit stand at the edge of the gravel. Several baskets of fruit waited in the shade for potential customers, along with a dozen Ball mason jars packed tight with rich brown apple butter. My empty stomach growled at the sight.

I was barely out of the car when I heard a shout from the house. "Hello!" cried a woman's voice. "Hello and good afternoon!"

"Hi." I shaded my eyes against the sun in time to see a woman get up from a porch swing and start toward me across the green lawn. She had long brown hair that fell halfway down her back, curling at the ends, and shot through by streaks of silver. I guessed her age at somewhere around fifty. She wore a loose denim sundress that bared her sunburned shoulders and legs that were long, slim, and younger than her face. Behind her square wire-framed glasses, her eyes were caught up in a nest of smile lines.

"Are you Ms. Crocker?" I asked.

"Nope," she replied. She stopped a couple of feet from me and bared a mouthful of white teeth. She was several inches taller than me, tall enough that she had to tilt her face down to talk to me. "I've never answered to such a name. I'm Corrie."

"My name is Savvy," I said. I thought for a moment about which last name to provide, then decided to skip it altogether. I didn't think Corrie would mind.

"Cool name," said the woman. She reached out, but instead of shaking my hand, she poked a finger against my arm. "And you're real!"

"Does that surprise you?" I asked. People had often doubted the authenticity of my stories, but this was the first time anyone had questioned my physical presence.

"Nothing surprises me much," said Corrie, "but considering some of the things I've seen in the last couple of days, I thought it wouldn't hurt to check."

"So you've been having the hallucinations, too?"

"Too?" Corrie chuckled. "You mean there was other people seeing things?"

I nodded. "All over the island. The Centers for Disease Control is in town. They think it's an epidemic."

"And here I was thinking it was only me." Corrie laughed again and shook her head, sending her long hair swinging around her shoulders. "I didn't always make the best decisions back in the sixties. I thought it was just a flashback."

I couldn't help but smile back at her. Unlike the bitter smiles I had received from Dr. Benedict, there was no trace of sarcasm in Corrie's expression. Though I had talked to the woman no more than a minute, I was already sure she could have nothing to do with poisoning the town. "Has anyone else been out here in the last couple of days?"

"Nope," Corrie replied. "Not that I would have noticed if they had been. I've been too busy chasing dinosaurs and elves around the woods." She turned toward the road and squinted. "I'm surprised there hasn't been more folks around. I get a pretty steady stream of customers up from St. Louis this time of year."

"The ferry's out," I said, making no mention of my part in ruining her trade.

She nodded. "That would explain it." She turned back to me, her bright green eyes studying my face. "Tell me about this epidemic. Is everyone all right?"

"There have been some injuries," I told her. I thought about mentioning the dead policeman, but decided to pass. As long as I couldn't produce a body, that observation only made me sound like one of the ergot eaters. "A girl named Jennifer Franklin is sick."

"Jenny?" Corrie frowned and shook her head. "That's a real shame. She was up here just before the Apple Festival. Seemed very excited to be home again."

"Back?" I thought of what Mayor Cullison had told me when we found Jenny. "I thought she had only been on the island a couple of days?"

Corrie nodded, pushing her glasses up her nose with one finger. "She has. But Jenny lived here when she was small. Her father used to be one of the biggest landowners on the island—sold me this farm better than fifteen years ago. But then he got in money trouble. Sold off near everything he had here and left for the mainland."

I smiled at the way the woman seemed to consider land less than half a mile from Meridian another country, but the information only added to the swirl of facts spinning around my skull. Everyone on Meridian seemed to be involved in some way in the life of everyone else. It was probably true of any community so small and isolated, but it didn't make things easy. I felt an urgent need for fourteen hours of solid sleep and a big organizational chart.

"Can I ask you some questions?" I asked.

"Seems like you already are," said Corrie. Her green eyes swept my face again. "You some kind of reporter?"

Sometimes I wondered if I had a tattoo on my forehead. "I work for a newspaper," I said with a nod. "I'm investigating what's going on."

Corrie turned away. Her sandled feet crunched across the gravel as she walked over to the fruit stand. "Sounds to me like you think there's more than germs going 'round this island."

"What makes you say that?"

"Because," she said, "if there was nothing but germs, you'd be back in town talking with these Disease Control people. If you're out here talking to me, you must think I've got something to tell you that those big bugs can't." She pulled a stool out from behind the stand and sat down, her bare legs swinging above the ground.

I was impressed. Corrie Crocker might look like the picture of an aging hippie, but there was a sharp mind behind her granny glasses. "I wanted to talk to you about Agrotex."

"Agrotex?" Corrie's mouth wrinkled as if she had bitten into a lemon. "Are they to blame for this disease?"

"Maybe." I walked over to the fruit stand and ran my hands over the rough wood. "I take it you're not too fond of Agrotex."

She tossed back her head and gave a bark of laughter. "You don't need to be so subtle. I think Agrotex is a technological horror filled with abominations of nature and run by people that wouldn't know organic fertilizer if they stepped in it."

"You were part of the protests against them?"

She nodded. "Damn straight. It wasn't just me. There's a lot of folks around here that don't want things like Agrotex moving in."

"People like Mayor Cullison?" I asked.

"Jordan's a good man." For the first time Corrie gave me a look that was less than friendly. "You're not saying he's done something wrong, are you?"

I shook my head quickly. "Not at all. I'm just trying to find out what's going on. Agrotex says they've had trouble with people breaking in."

This information seemed to surprise her. "It wasn't me, I can promise you that much. And I don't believe anyone I know would have been involved." She paused and sighed. "If it wasn't for that Hoffman woman going and getting herself killed, we wouldn't be having all these troubles."

I ran the name through my memory, but came up with no matches. However, the words *killed* and *trouble* in the same sentence seemed too good to pass up. "Who was she?" I asked. "How did she die?"

Corrie shrugged. "Don't know her first name. She came in here about ten years back and bought up a few acres of what used to be Franklin land. We didn't think much of it at the time. She was quiet and kept to herself. Nobody paid any attention till she went out and bought that damn boat."

I wasn't sure just where this story was going, but I was willing to chase it a little farther. "What kind of boat?"

"Couldn't even properly call it a boat," said Corey. "That thing was big enough to be a yacht."

"So this Hoffman woman was rich?"

Corrie shrugged. "Nobody around here thought so. She lived simple enough till she come up with the boat."

"What happened to her."

"Not two weeks after she got that boat, she ran smack into a grain barge." She slapped her hands together. "Went down like a stone. Then, before anyone could even think about it, Agrotex rode down to the probate court and snatched up the land. They had that farm in there before the Hoffman woman was cold in the ground."

I put the story together in my mind. Mysterious woman moves into an isolated community. She lives cheaply, then displays sudden wealth. She dies, and Agrotex is Johnny on the spot to grab her land. It wasn't clear to me yet how any of this fit with what had been going on in Meridian over the last couple of days, but I had a strong suspicion that there was a connection to be discovered.

"I heard you were part of a group called Meridian Is Our Home."

"That's right," Corrie said with a nod. She looked at me with one eyebrow raised above the rim of her glasses. "Someone tell you we're a bunch of crackpots out to turn off the lights and drive all the cars into the river?"

"Not quite," I replied. "Was it Agrotex that got you started? Did you organize to stop them from building their station?"

Corrie shook her head. "Nope, we'd already been around for years. Every year or so some city-side developer notices that this is one of the few islands out here that's high enough to avoid the floods and close enough to the city to be worth something." She stood up from her stool and smoothed out her denim dress. "Come on down to the riverbank with me, I'll show you where Home got started."

I followed her around the sprawling two-story house and down a grassy slope. Through a leaning line of oaks and poplars, the brown water of the Mississippi came into view. Along the shoreline was a beach made up of dark rounded stones and the white interiors of empty mussel shells. Corrie walked over the slippery rocks with confidence, then stopped beside an odd construction. It was a low concrete pen, perhaps twenty feet across and no more than three feet high, with the rusted metal remains of heavy reinforcing rods jutting out on all sides.

She nodded at the mud-stained wall. "This is where Home began," she said. "This was our big victory."

I stared at the ugly low construction. It didn't seem to be a big anything. "What is that?"

"It was going to be the footing for a bridge," said Corrie. She raised her hand and pointed at the distant Illinois bank of the river. "They were going to run from the state highway over there straight out to Meridian. My house and most of my orchard would have been plowed under for blacktop." She turned to me, determination stamped on her tan face. "Jordan was the one that got us organized. He put a stop to the bridge."

I took a few steps toward the river and looked out over the surging water. Jordan Cullison was certainly an unusual mayor. In most towns, a mayor was expected to cheer progress at any price. Yet Cullison had been elected after stopping the biggest project in the island's history. It said a lot about the man, and even more about the community.

"Corrie," I said as I turned around. "What about the Apple Festival, were you . . . were you—" I stopped as I realized that the orchard owner was not paying attention to me. She was staring at the stump of the bridge piling with a stunned expression that reminded me of fishes lying on ice at the grocery store.

I walked closer and stood on tiptoe to see over the wall. The inside of the piling was filled with water and rimmed with a thick layer of green algae.

Floating in this little riverside pond were two bodies. One was the missing policeman, the second was Cap'n Finley.

THIRTEEN

CORRIE CROCKER LEANED AGAINST ME AS WE WALKED BACK UP the hill to her home. "They're dead," she moaned.

I couldn't argue with that. "It'll be all right," I said. Of course, it wouldn't be all right, but it was the best I could think of at that moment.

"I can't believe they're dead," said Corrie. She stopped in her tracks, spun around, and clutched at me, pulling me into a tight hug as her chest heaved with sobs.

It would have been a good deal less awkward if Corrie had not been several inches taller than me. As it was, her chin ground against the top of my head and her thick hair fell down across my face like a blanket.

"Let's just get away from here," I suggested, my voice muffled as I spoke through the screen of hair.

"Poor Tom Macavoy," said Corrie. She began a fresh round of sobbing.

I reached around her as best I could and patted her on the back. "He must have been a good friend."

She pulled away from me and shook her head. "He was an arrogant jerk! He was in favor of the bridge, and Agrotex, and everything that would bring in a buck. But he didn't deserve this." She took off her glasses and wiped at her eyes. "And poor Pete Finley, he drank a bit more than he should, but you never met a sweeter man."

I couldn't testify to the sweetness that Corrie mentioned, but I did feel a guilty relief that I would never have to explain to the man how I lost his boat. "Let's get up to the house," I said. "I'll have to go into town and let someone know about the bodies."

Corrie sniffed back tears and nodded. "You're right," she said. "The important thing now is finding who did this." With that, she spun around and started up the hill at a quick march, her moment of weakness apparently behind her.

As I followed her up the grassy bank I thought about the position of the bodies. The bridge piling was an isolated location. If Corrie hadn't taken me down to talk about Home's victory over the Illinois State Highway Department, the bodies could have lain there undiscovered for months—maybe forever.

It was a location that must surely be known to only a few people on the island—including Mayor Cullison. Macavoy had been one of the proponents of progress on the island. If Mayor Cullison or one of the other island environmentalists was behind the insanity, then there might be some reason for the police officer's death. It was a weak motive, and if there was a connection between the policeman and the ferry pilot, I sure didn't see it, but it was the best idea I had at the moment.

As we topped the hill beside Corrie's house I glanced over at the swing on her front porch. It looked like a wonderfully pleasant place to sit, catch the breeze coming across the orchard, and look out over the treetops to where you could spot tugboats moving along the wide river. It was terrible to think that someone had wanted to tear this place down to make way for a new highway.

In the middle of this reverie, I spotted something beside the swing that made me grab Corrie by the hand and pull her to a stop. "Corrie, is that an apple core?" I asked, pointing to the porch.

She followed the direction of my finger and nodded. "Two of them. Why? You concerned about my house-cleaning habits?"

I pulled her around to face me. "When did you eat those apples?"

"Just before you got here," she replied. She raised an eyebrow. "There's plenty more if you want one."

"No," I said. "It's not that. According to Dr. Benedict, the apples are the source of the disease. They're infected with a fungus that makes people go crazy."

Corrie grunted in disgust. "Maybe some of those apples that have been sprayed with God knows what," she said, "but not my apples."

I stared into her eyes. Corrie wasn't acting strangely, or talking about any hallucination, and her pupils didn't seem to be dilated—if that was even a symptom of ergot ingestion. "Are these the first apples you ate today?" I asked.

She shook her head. "I had another before breakfast. My apples are the best on the island, you can ask anyone. That's why they always use them at the festival."

I felt my mouth drop open, then closed it quickly. I let go of Corrie's hand, ran over to the fruit stand, and picked up an apple. The afternoon sun was shining brightly down on the parking lot. I held the apple up to the light and looked at it closely. There were no black spots.

"These apples aren't infected," I said.

"Told you," Corrie replied.

The apples grown at this farm were clean, but the apple that had come from the Apple Festival had been infested with ergot. It had to mean that I was right on at least one point: these apples had not been infected by this mold while they were on the trees; the poison had been deliberately introduced sometime after they had been picked. The mystery in Meridian was not a matter of an unforeseen consequence of agricultural experimentation, it was deliberate poisoning—and murder.

From up the road came the sound of motors. I looked up to see a pair of white vehicles come sweeping into the parking area. The first vehicle was a Jeep with the markings of the CDC on the doors. The second was an unmarked panel van.

Corrie stepped up beside me. "Looks like the marines have arrived," she said.

The doors on the lead car opened, but the two

figures inside had a hard time climbing out. Both were wearing the white bubble suits and helmets, and the clumsy gear made it difficult to deal with seat belts and small doors. Right away I recognized the driver of the vehicle as my pal Buzz Cut from back at the clinic. He stomped toward us while the passenger continued to struggle with his door.

"You don't look like you've come for an apple," Corrie said to the man.

He marched straight past her and stopped in front of me. "You're Savvy Skye," he growled.

I winced. "Yeah, I guess I am."

Buzz Cut leaned over me, his face beet red inside the helmet. "Do you know what the penalty is for lying to a CDC official in a medical crisis?"

"No."

He stared at me for a moment longer, his upper lip quivering with anger. "Neither do I," he spat out at last. "But I'm certainly going to find out."

Corrie picked up a jar of apple butter and thumped it none too gently against the side of the man's helmet. Buzz Cut stumbled back a step and turned to her in surprise. "What are you doing?" he demanded.

"Back off, big boy," Corrie warned him. Her green eyes flared. "You behave yourself or you'll get your chance to breathe unfiltered air with the rest of us."

There was a squeak of flexing rubber as the man's hands tightened into fists. "I'm Colonel James Harriman," he said. "I'm in charge of this operation."

Corrie took a step toward him, putting her face only inches from his helmet. "This is not an operation, this is an orchard—*my* orchard. And as long as this is the

United States of America, I expect visitors to my property to behave themselves."

Colonel Harriman snarled, but he backed away. "This is an emergency situation."

The second passenger of the white Jeep finally managed to get free of entanglements and approached across the gravel. At first I thought it was another of the CDC workers, but as he came closer the face inside the helmet made my mouth drop open in surprise.

"Jimmy?"

Jimmy Knoles grinned from behind the glass plate. "We have to stop meeting like this."

"When did we ever meet like this before?"

"Never," he admitted, "but it seemed like a good opening line."

I shook my head slowly. "I don't believe this. What are you doing here?"

"I heard about the epidemic on the news," Jimmy replied. "I remembered that you said you were going to Meridian and I got a little worried. So I pulled a few strings, pushed a few buttons, and fast-talked my way into a helicopter ride so I could come out to see you." He tapped his hand against the side of his helmet. "Not that we're going to get particularly intimate on this visit."

For a few moments I stood in silent amazement. The same guy that had told me things were moving too fast, the guy who had been afraid to spend a weekend with me, had turned around and gone through a tremendous effort to get to me when he thought I was in trouble. "You didn't know what was happening here," I said. "You could have been exposing yourself to something deadly."

Jimmy shrugged. "I knew you were here. I had to come get you."

"Damn, honey," said Corrie. "I think this one's a keeper."

I blushed and reached out to take Jimmy's gloved hand. "You didn't have to come, but thanks."

"No problem," he replied, but I could see that his cheeks were also red inside the helmet. He cleared his throat. "Besides, it looks like I made a mistake in coming. If I had just waited another hour, they would have probably brought you to me."

"What?" I looked over at Harriman. "I thought you put the island under quarantine."

"I did," said Colonel Buzz Cut. "And now I'm calling for an evacuation of all people on the island. Everyone is being moved to a CDC facility south of Moline."

"But why?" I asked. "Didn't Dr. Benedict tell you about the ergot? There's no disease here to catch, it's only a kind of fungus."

"Dr. Benedict has made his theory known," said the colonel. "But at this point that's all it is—a theory. We have no confirmation of it. Even if the disease is ergot, we need to get the patients to better treatment facilities before the secondary symptoms set in."

"Secondary symptoms?" Benedict had told me about the insanity, but he made no mention that there was a round two on the way.

Harriman suddenly grabbed hold of my right hand

and turned my palm up. "Poisoning by ergot alkaloids leads to gangrene of the extremities."

I pulled my hand away. "I don't have gangrene. I haven't even had any hallucinations."

He smiled. "So far."

"Wait a minute," said Corrie. She stepped around in front of Harriman. "You're telling me that whatever gave me that bad spell yesterday could rot off my arms and legs?"

Harriman nodded. "Potentially."

Corrie shook her head. "I don't have much use for you, but I've got a lot of use for my legs. Let's get going." She shoved past the colonel and started toward the van.

Harriman turned to me. "Time for you to leave as well, Ms. Skye, or McKinnon, or whatever your name is."

"Just a minute." I grabbed Jimmy by the arm and pulled him aside. "You've got to do something for me," I whispered. "Have you got a cell phone I can borrow?"

Jimmy smiled through the glass. "Don't tell me. You've got a big story and you want me to act as your research mule."

I squeezed his hand. "Would you, please?"

He rolled his eyes. "You break your neck to save someone's life, and all they want is more. All right, I've got a phone in the Jeep you can use. Just tell me what you want."

"That's great." I thought for a second. Then dropped my voice to a low whisper. "There are two dead bodies at the bottom of the hill."

"What!" Jimmy shouted, then he caught himself and lowered his voice. "Savvy, if this disease is killing people, then you have to tell the CDC."

"I don't think this disease had anything to do with the deaths. At least one of the two was killed by bullets." I looked around to make sure that Harriman was standing out of earshot then went on. "I think someone is using all this to cover up a murder."

"Good God." Jimmy shook his head. "You need to get out of here now. Anyone that would go to this kind of extreme is not going to be upset at having to kill one more."

"I'll get out," I said. "As soon as I have my story. One of the dead men down there is the ferry pilot that brought me over here. His name is Pete Finley. The other one is a policeman from Meridian named Tom Macavoy. Can you check them out for me?"

"Finley and Macavoy." Jimmy nodded. "Is there more?"

I put my hand against my forehead. "There's too much more. I also need information on a company called Agrotex. Who owns it, where did they come from, and what do they do?"

"Got it. What else?"

"A few more names to check out. Jennifer Franklin, and her father—sorry, I don't have his first name."

"You're not making this easy for me," said Jimmy, "but I'll try. Anyone else?"

I nodded. "Jordan Cullison—he's the mayor of Meridian—and Frederick Benedict, the town doctor."

Jimmy shook his head. "That's a pretty long list of suspects, Savvy. Any minute now someone's going to

ship you out of this place. I don't think you're going to
solve this before they send you packing."

"Just get me what information you can," I said. I
stood on tiptoe and planted a kiss on his face shield.
After two days there was no trace of lipstick, but still
I left a satisfying lip print behind.

Jimmy reached out and hugged me against the bulky
suit. "When we get home, we're going to have to talk."

"You better believe it," I said.

Harriman shuffled our way. "It's time to break it up
and get this show on the road."

I gave Jimmy a last squeeze and followed him over
to the car. He fished inside and came out with the
cellular phone, holding it clumsily in his gloved hand.
"I'll call as soon as I find what you want," he said.

"Save your money," said Harriman. "By the time
you place a call, all of us will be off this island." He
climbed into the vehicle and closed the door.

I took the phone from Jimmy. "Call when you can.
I'll be here."

Jimmy shook his head. "I know you want to get
your story, but get out of here as soon as you can," he
said. "And be *careful*."

I ran my fingers quickly across my chest. "Cross my
heart."

Jimmy climbed into the Jeep and it sped the parking
area in a shower of gravel. Leaving Dr. Benedict's blue
sedan behind, I walked around to the back of the van.
More suited figures opened the door and let me in to
sit on a long bench seat next to Corrie. Thick plates of
glass separated the driver from us contaminated folks
in the back.

"Sorry if I put a crimp in your plans," Corrie said as they slammed the door behind me. "I don't like the idea of being hauled away from home, but I'm also fond of walking."

"I can't blame you for that." I dropped onto the cushion and eyed the empty bench across the aisle. It looked just long enough and just soft enough to allow a short nap.

"How long has that Jimmy been yours?" Corrie asked.

"He's not mine, really," I said. "Not yet anyway. He thinks he's too old for me."

Corrie leaned over and whispered in my ear. "Don't let him shake you. This difference in your ages doesn't mean a thing."

"You really think so?"

She nodded. "Of course. My husband was twenty years older than me. He was a professor, and I was a grad student." She lowered her voice to a whisper. "Best sex I ever had. A very experienced man, my husband." She leaned back and smiled a sad, wistful sigh. "Too bad it had to end."

I laid a hand on her arm. "Did he die?"

Corrie shook her head. "Nope. The day I hit thirty-five he ran off with a sophomore." She closed her eyes and leaned back in her seat, a smile still on her lips. "Son-of-a-bitch never could stop chasing the young ones."

FOURTEEN

THE WORDS ON THE SIDE OF THE GYM READ HOME OF THE APPLE
Corps. It was, I suppose, a clever title for a school that
must have had barely enough kids to fill a basketball
team. Equally impressive was the line of huge twin-
rotor helicopters parked in the softball field.

"Abernathy through Baxter," said a voice over a
loudspeaker. "Abernathy through Baxter move to position one."

A small knot of people broke away from the crowds
waiting along the third-base line and walked toward
the first of the choppers. The evacuation of Meridian
was under way.

"Bolivar through Crocker," blared the loudspeaker.
"Bolivar through Crocker to position two."

Corrie gave me a quick hug. "I guess this is where
I get on the bus," she said.

"Good luck," I said.

She looked down at her own hands. "I don't see any
gangrene. If they put me through all this and it turns

out I'm fine, I am going to be royally pissed." With that, she trudged out onto the field and joined the others waiting beside the second helicopter.

As soon as she was gone, I stretched my neck and looked around. There was no sign of either Jimmy or Terry. It had been almost an hour since we had left Corrie's farm, and still there was no call. I was starting to believe that Harriman was right—I would be off Meridian before I got a chance to stop the killer.

At the far end of the line, I spotted a tall dark figure looming over the crowd. It was a welcome sight. I broke ranks with the rest of the Hullings through Miller pack and pushed my way down the line.

"Dr. Kumal!" I called, waving to the station director.

Kumal looked my way and nodded. "Ms. Skye."

I stopped in front of the big man and looked up into his dark eyes. "I see Agrotex personnel are also being evacuated."

"Yes," he replied with a nod. "Agrotex is cooperating fully with this operation. After all, we have nothing to hide."

"I'm sure you don't," I said.

The bullhorn crackled into life again. "Darling through Holman," called the amplified voice. "Darling through Holman to position three." More people broke away and began to walk across the field. Already the number remaining on the line was beginning to look a little thin.

Kumal folded his muscled arms. "I've already answered your questions, Ms. Skye" he said. "Any further inquiries should be handled through the Agrotex public-relations department. I'll be happy to provide you with the number."

I nodded. "I appreciate that." I wished we had a place to sit down. Looking up to Dr. Kumal's lofty elevation was beginning to hurt my neck. "But these questions don't really have anything to do with Agrotex."

The director's brow furrowed. "What did you want to ask?"

"It's about the woman that lived there before you built your farm. Do you know anything about her?"

Kumal was quiet for a moment. "Very little," he said at last. "I wasn't involved in the negotiations to buy the land."

"But you must have heard something," I insisted.

He let out one of his rumbling sighs. "I hate to repeat rumors," he said. "But I did hear that the woman was engaged to a scientist of some sort—a chemist, I believe. But the man had become a criminal. He was in jail for a serious offense."

Criminal was good. It seemed to reinforce my idea that the dead woman had a connection to the murders and madness. Scientist was even better. It would take someone with some scientific knowledge to pull off the ersatz epidemic in Meridian.

"What kind of crimes did he commit?" I asked. "Do you know?"

The doctor's answer was interrupted by the bellow of the loudspeaker. "Hullings through Miller, position four. Hullings through Miller to position four."

Kumal stepped away. "I'm afraid it's time for me to leave."

I hurried to keep up with him. "What about the crimes?" I asked as we neared the helicopter. "Murder? Assault?"

The director paused a dozen paces from the last of the huge helicopters. "No," he said. "I believe it was embezzlement."

The answer stopped me. Embezzlement was not exactly my idea of a major crime. These days it seemed that every third banker was accused of embezzlement and at least half of them were convicted. As far as I knew, none of them had felt compelled to poison a whole town.

I stood there in the grass while Kumal climbed into the chopper, then I slowly walked back across the field to the sidelines. I edged through the people that remained, looking for someone else to talk to, until I reached the space-suited figure holding up the left end of the line. I was pleased to see that the face behind the glass belonged to Kirin Havers.

"Hi," I called to her.

Kirin seemed less than happy to see me. "You lied to me," she said.

"Not really, I just—" I stopped and bit my lip. "All right, I lied to you. I'm sorry."

"I could have really gotten in trouble," said Kirin.

"Sorry," I repeated. "I wouldn't have done it if I didn't think it was important. Have you seen my friend?"

"The one from the clinic? The cute one?"

I should have known she would be keeping track of Terry. "That's the one."

"He and the doctor are still at the clinic, taking care

of that girl that's sick. The poor thing's scheduled to go out on the very last flight." Kirin shook her head sadly. "I'm not sure she's going to make it."

"I need to go over to the clinic," I said.

"No way," Kirin replied promptly. "You've got to stay here and go out with the rest of them." Her frown grew deeper. "Isn't your name McKinnon? You're supposed to be getting loaded on right now."

"I can't go. There's been a murder."

Kirin blinked in surprise. "A murder?"

I nodded. "Actually, it's two murders."

"Two?" Kirin frowned and her eyes narrowed to slits. "I'm not sure I believe you. You already lied to me once."

"You'll just have to trust me."

For a moment she seemed to be considering it. Then she shook her head sharply. "Not this time," she said. "Everything is already planned out."

"But—"

"No," she said. "You're getting on that helicopter. There's no point in talking about it anymore."

Behind me, the loudspeaker rumbled to life again. "If your name has been called, please board quickly. Transports will be departing in a few moments."

I looked at Kirin and nodded. "I guess you're right. There's no point in talking about it." I turned toward the fields and took off running as fast as I could go.

"Wait!" came a shout from Kirin.

Other voices joined in. I glanced over my shoulder and saw several of the white figures moving my way, but they were encumbered by their suits and I outdistanced them quickly. For someone that had always

been the slowest kid in gym class, it was an exhila-
rating feeling.

I ran across the corner of the softball field, dashed
through the parking lot of a gas station, and emerged
into a long green lawn behind the church. By that point
the CDC personnel were out of sight, and I was out of
breath. I slowed to a walk, holding a hand against a
stitch in my side.

Something vibrated at my waist. I jumped, then
looked down to see Jimmy's phone hanging from my
belt. Evidently, it was set for a silent ring. I stopped in
the shadow of the church, pulled up the antenna, and
pressed the button.

"Jimmy?"

I got an earful of static, then Jimmy's voice came
through very faintly. "Savvy? Are you there?"

"I'm here!" I shouted into the phone. "I'm not
picking up very well. Did you find anything to connect
Macavoy and Finley?"

"Not a thing. Finley had a number of drunk-and-
disorderly arrests. Macavoy was clean. I'm looking at
the phone . . ."

A helicopter lifted from the ball field and moved
over Meridian. The heavy beat of its rotors momentarily drowned out the weak sound from the phone.

"Savvy?" Jimmy said again after the chopper had
gone past. "Can you hear me?"

"I'm here," I said. "It's a little noisy in these parts."

There was another blast of static, then Jimmy came
through again. ". . . not such a nice guy."

"Who?"

"What?" said Jimmy.

"Who wasn't a nice guy?" I bellowed into the handset.

"Franklin," Jimmy replied. "You told me to track down Jennifer Franklin's father. Well, I found him. His name's Albert Franklin and he used to own half the docks between Alton and St. Louis. It looks like he did a lot of business from those docks that wasn't strictly legal. In fact, I'm not sure any of it was legal. The man had a reputation for being a pretty tough customer."

"I thought Franklin was still alive," I replied.

"He is. But he's retired from the game. Fifteen years ago he got involved in the precious metals market. It was a time when prices were going through the roof. It looks like Franklin was using the metal purchases as part of some kind of money-laundering scheme." Static drowned out the next few seconds, then: ". . . spent some time in jail."

"Franklin went to jail?"

"No!" said Jimmy. "Arnold went to jail. Just got out about six months ago."

"Who's Arnold?"

"Monk Arnold. He was one of Franklin's partners. Talked Franklin into buying more than five million dollars in platinum right before the bottom fell out of the market. Only someone else took him to the cleaners. They never recovered the . . ."

Jimmy's voice trailed away into static, and this time it didn't return. I held the phone to my ear and waited, hoping for another call, but the little cell phone was silent. After a few minutes I gave up and returned it to my belt.

Leaving the protective shadows of the church, I started up the street toward the clinic. The sun was getting very low in the west. It hung just above the roofs of the small cluster of shops that made up downtown Meridian. The light it cast over the silent town was red, almost bloody. The first time I had entered Meridian there had been a frightening feeling that danger was lurking behind every window. That feeling was gone now. In only a few hours the town gone mad had been transformed into something sad and empty. I walked slowly along the deserted street, feeling every hour of the day settling in my exhausted muscles.

The snippets of information that had filtered through the static of Jimmy's call were enough to fill in a few gaps. Albert Franklin had owned a lot of land in Meridian before Monk Arnold had scammed him in a precious-metals scheme. Arnold had spent time in jail. If he was the same man who had been the dead Ms. Hoffman's fiancé, then I had my connection to the Agrotex property.

The clinic was strangely dark and quiet as I walked up the short flight of stairs. The plastic-and-tape walls still hung in the front room, but the process of moving out people and equipment had left them tattered. Loose curls of tape dangled from the ceiling tiles and pieces of torn plastic lay scattered on the floor. Without the lights on, the whole place had the feel of a cheap carnival funhouse gone to seed.

I had just stepped inside when I heard a sound from up the street. A vehicle was approaching. I stuck my head back through the door, expecting to see one of the white CDC vehicles on its way. Instead I saw a tan wagon approaching—Mayor Cullison's wagon.

At once, something that Cullison had said back at the fairgrounds echoed in my skull. He had worked for Franklin. He had even said something about talking to Franklin again.

I pulled my head back and stood in the shadows of the front room while Cullison stopped his car and climbed out. In the fading sunlight, the bearded mayor looked more than a little sinister. He was a big man, powerfully built. There were dark stains across his clothing I hadn't seen before.

Moving away from the door, I ducked past one of the sheets of hanging plastic and bounced off a fallen chair. "Terry?" I called quietly into the darkness. "Terry, are you in here?"

A car door slammed outside. Cullison was coming.

I stumbled on through the dark room, pushing through one diving sheet after another. Cullison had worked for Albert Franklin and he had a connection to the Agrotex property. Cullison might also have a link to Monk Arnold. He might even be working for Franklin or Arnold. There were just too many things I didn't know, and in this kind of situation, what you didn't know could kill you.

I banged my hip against a table and nearly tripped over a stack of empty boxes. Cullison knew about Agrotex and the fungus. A sheet of plastic fell down over my head, and I clawed it out of the way. Cullison had been missing all day—plenty of time to move two bodies to a place he probably knew better than anyone else on the island.

My breath was coming hard by the time I came to an actual wooden door. I grabbed the knob, flung it open, and ran smack into someone standing in a darkened hallway.

I staggered back, then looked up to see the tall form of a powerfully built man. In his right hand he held the gleaming form of a knife poised to strike.

An involuntary squeak of fear escaped through my lips. "Don't!"

"Savvy?" said a familiar voice. "You okay?"

"Terry." Relief hit me so hard I almost fell over. "What are you doing here?"

He shrugged his wide shoulders and took a step back. Pale light from the front windows showed that the knife in his hands was actually a pair of scissors. "I was just getting ready to help with Jenny. We're going to have to move her."

From the lobby I heard the door open and shut.

"Come on," I whispered to Terry. "We've got to go."

"Why?" he asked in a maddeningly loud voice.

A shadow moved behind the translucent walls. "Just go," I whispered. I put my hands against his back and shoved him along the hall to the back room.

Terry craned his neck to look behind us. "Who are we running from?"

"Mayor Cullison."

"Why? I like the mayor."

"So do I, but he might be the killer." I shut the door

at the end of the hallway. "And we don't want to be next."

The back room of the clinic was almost as deserted as the front. Only a single dying patient remained. In one corner of the room Jenny Franklin lay on a table, flanked by a panel of flashing LEDs. She looked worse than ever. Her eyes were sunken and surrounded by deep gray shadows. Her chest rose and fell in jerky, convulsive movements. Her erratic breathing sounded spooky in the quiet room.

"Where's the doctor?" I whispered.

Terry shrugged. "I think he went to get more insulin from one of the storerooms. Jenny's really doing bad."

"Okay," I said. "You stay here and watch her. I'm going to go find Dr. Benedict, and then we're all going to get out of here."

Moving as quietly as my leather-soled shoes would allow, I edged past Jenny's bed and headed for the line of storage rooms. The first room, where Benedict had shown me the contaminated apple, was dark. The door to the next was closed. I tapped on it softly.

"Dr. Benedict? Are you in here?"

I took hold of the knob and eased the door open a crack. The CDC had apparently avoided using this room. There were only a pair of locked cabinets, a small table topped by a shiny metal bowl, and an odd medical device leaning in the corner.

Something brushed against my hip. I jumped into the room and backed up against the wall. Only when my side was prodded for a second time did I realize that it was Jimmy's phone ringing again. I snatched the device from my belt and tugged out the antenna.

"Jimmy?"

"Hi, Savvy." The connection was better this time, though the sound was full of the usual car-phone crackle. "The CDC folks tell me you missed your taxi."

"You know how it is," I replied as loudly as I dared. "There's always some last-minute item to take care of. Did you find out anything about Jordan Cullison?"

There was a pause and the sound of shuffling papers. "I couldn't find much," Jimmy said at last. "He dropped out of college his junior year. One citation for pot about a year before that."

"Nothing else?"

"Nope," Jimmy replied. "And that's still more than I've got on Benedict. I haven't been able to find him in any database."

There was a noise in the hallway.

"Gotta go," I whispered into the phone. I hung up and backed into the corner, crouching down to put the table between myself and the door. As I did I bumped into the device in the corner. It slid along the wall and toppled with a resounding bang.

Only after it was on the ground did I realize that the thing was not a piece of medical gear—it was a metal detector. I dropped Jimmy's phone on the table and picked up the detector. It was clear the machine had been used, and used recently. Mud still clung to the coils at the bottom. Looking at that mud, I saw a trio of holes in the dark earth of a wheat field, and the coppery gleam of an underground sprinkler.

There was a click from the doorway, and the small

room was suddenly flooded in light. "I see you found my little toy," said Dr. Benedict.

I looked from the metal detector to the man in the doorway. "You're Monk Arnold."

He nodded. "And you're so smart I'm going to have to kill you."

FIFTEEN

THE PHONY DOCTOR SIGHED AND SHOOK HIS HEAD. "PEOPLE never know what's good for them," he said. "I give you a perfectly good story, and you have to go and throw it away." He stood casually, his hands jammed into the pockets of his coat. As a doctor, he had seemed insufferably rude. Revealed as a killer, he appeared much more relaxed.

"It was you that dug up the Agrotex wheat fields," I said.

He nodded. "That part's obvious."

"But you never found the platinum, did you?"

"Not yet." Benedict eased the door closed and leaned against it. "But there should be over two hundred kilograms remaining. I'm confident that if I get a little time to myself, I'll have no trouble locating it."

"And you grew the ergot fungus."

"Guilty," he agreed with a grin. Freed of the persona

of Dr. Frederick Benedict, even his features seemed to have shifted. His eyes were colder, the corner of his mouth adopted a twist that was almost a leer. "I needed some way to clear out the Agrotex farm. A little natural LSD and a lot of fast talking seemed like just the ticket to get everyone out of here and make double sure the Agrotex complex was empty."

I tightened my grip on the shaft of the metal detector. "You swindled Albert Franklin and hid the platinum on his land."

Arnold frowned. "I thought I said that already." He shook his head. "This conversation is getting boring."

I put the next few steps together as fast as I could think of them. "You left your girlfriend to watch over the stash, but she got herself killed before you got out."

The killer's frown deepened. "If she could have held the purse shut for a few months longer, we'd both be sailing along the Riviera right now. But she had to be an idiot and blow a block of cash on that damn boat."

"And you came out of prison to find Agrotex sitting on your money. So you assumed the name of Frederick Benedict while you waited for your chance to get your money."

"You know," said Arnold, "you're really very good at this. I am disappointed that you didn't mention the little joke in the names. Arnold. Benedict. Benedict Arnold. I thought that was particularly clever."

I forced myself to smile. "Very nice. But then Tom

Macavoy figured out who you were and you had to kill him."

Arnold shook his head. "That cop would never have figured out who I was in a million years. It was the girl."

"Jenny Franklin?"

He nodded. "She saw me when she came into town. Remembered me from when she was a kid. She wasn't sure, but she went running to Macavoy." He laughed. "It's a good thing Macavoy was stupid enough to come to me before he starting checking the records. Otherwise I might never have had a chance to stop him."

"What about Captain Finley?" I asked. "He was no cop. What did you have against him?"

"Nothing," said Arnold. "I liked old Finley."

"Then why did you kill him?"

Arnold shrugged. "I didn't start out to kill him. It was you I was after."

"Me?"

"Saw your lights when you drove onto the island," he replied. "I went up to dear Mrs. Myrtle's house to see who it was. Finley popped out of your car while I was making sure you didn't do any more driving, and, well . . . I'm afraid I acted rather rashly." He held up a finger and mimed a gunshot.

While Arnold talked I slowly raised the metal detector up to my waist and tilted it to the side. "So you killed them both. And the ergot was all just a cover story."

He clucked his tongue. "Things didn't go quite how

I planned. I've been culturing the ergot for months. I was going to spread it around the farm, get them to close the place down. Then the girl showed up and put the pressure on. But thanks to the wonderful CDC, I've still got plenty of time to dig up my loot."

It wasn't until then that I realized the last bit of the picture. A fresh chill went down my spine. "Jenny Franklin's not a diabetic."

"Sadly no," said Arnold. "Funny, one little five-dollar bracelet, and I've got a perfect murder. If I had come up with this idea sooner, my whole life could have been so much smoother."

I raised the metal detector over my head and swung for the fences.

Arnold stepped back with surprising speed. The round coils of the detector cut the air an inch away from his nose, but the killer was, sadly, unharmed. His right hand slipped out of his pocket with an ungainly ball of wrinkled aluminum foil clutched between his fingers.

"Drop the detector," he said.

I looked at the thing in his hand. It was the same mass of foil I had seen him carrying the first night on the island. "What are you going to do with that?" I asked. "Seal in freshness?"

He smiled a very undoctorly smile. "Very funny. There's a Glock nine-millimeter inside this foil. If it goes off—when it goes off—you won't ever have to worry about making another smart remark."

I took a step back, my eyes fixed on the wrinkled silver lump. "What are you going to do with that?"

"What do you think?" asked Arnold. He raised the lump and directed the barrel of the hidden gun my way.

There was a knock at the door. "Savvy? Are you in there?"

"Terry!" I screamed. "Benedict's the killer! He's got a gun!"

The door flew open, smashing against Benedict's back. At the same moment the gun went off.

The sound alone was almost loud enough to knock me down. Hot bits of aluminum foil peppered my left cheek and the bullet smashed into the paneling over my head.

Terry charged into the room with absolutely no trace of dimples in his expression. He shoved the door open so fast that Benedict was sent spinning.

The phony doctor growled and pointed his foil-wrapped pistol at Terry.

That's when I raised the metal detector and took my second swing. The round coils clipped Arnold on the jaw. He staggered back, dropped the pistol to the ground, and folded up like a cheap umbrella.

Terry looked at me. "Are you okay, Savvy?"

"Yeah," I said. "I'm good." I fought down a batch of giggles. The combination of exhaustion and relief was more intoxicating than a case of champagne. "Girl's softball team ninth and tenth grade."

"What?"

I dropped the metal detector on top of the fallen killer. "Never mind. Tell me, is there anything in your strange-phenomenon books about ergot?"

Terry smiled and nodded enthusiastically. "Sure. There was this village in France where everybody went crazy." His blue eyes widened. "Hey, you don't think . . ."

SIXTEEN

EDITOR BILL GENOVESE DROPPED THE STACK OF PAPERS AND shook his head. "Where's the monster?"

"What?" I asked around a mouthful of fries.

"I send you out of town, I expect a monster," said the editor. "Or at least a good UFO. And where's the information on the rest of these cold-call reports? You never even talked to most of them."

I took a big bite of a double cheeseburger and shrugged. "No monster," I said. "And I didn't get a chance to talk to the people that called in, but you get a fake doctor, genetically engineered wheat, and a whole town gone mad."

Mr. Genovese pursed his lips and nodded. "All right, I can work with that." He looked at me and adopted his usual scowl. "Do you think you can stop eating long enough to finish this meeting?"

I put down the cheeseburger and wiped secret-recipe sauce away from my lips. "Sorry. I haven't eaten anything in almost three days. Between running all over Meridian and spending ten hours waiting for the CDC to decide I wasn't a threat to mankind, I nearly starved."

"I see." Mr. Genovese turned his attention back to the papers. "No monster," he grumbled softly.

"They can't all be monsters," I said, eyeing the rest of my fries.

The editor shook his head. "Obviously you're not looking at this thing in the right light. Sometimes the monster's just a little harder to find."

I stood up and stretched. "If you don't mind, I'd kind of like to get going."

"Oh?" Mr. Genovese looked at me over the top of the papers. "Are you in a hurry to get back to your desk, Ms. McKinnon?"

I leaned on his desk. "I just spent my whole weekend chasing down a killer on an island full of mad people. Surely you can give me the afternoon off?"

"This is a business day," said Mr. Genovese. "And it's not the policy of the *Global Query* to award comp time."

"But—"

Mr. Genovese cut me off. "But in this case, I'll make an exception." His underused facial muscles pulled his lips up into something that was almost a smile. "This is a good story. You can come in and edit it tomorrow."

His enthusiasm, though it was hardly overwhelming, staggered me. "Great," I said. "That's great." I took another bite of burger, gathered up the rest of my food, and headed for the door.

"Ms. McKinnon," he called after me.

I paused at the door and looked back. "Yes, Sir?"

"What do you think about '*Mad Doctor Drives Town Insane*'. Or maybe '*Mushrooms Make Meridian Mad*'." His frown returned, and he shook his head. "Neither one sounds right to me. They just don't have that zing."

I chewed a few fries and waited for vitamin grease to start the wheels in my tired brain. "Keep the insanity part," I said at last. "Then add Illinois."

" 'Insane, Illinois,' " Mr. Genovese said slowly. "Or better yet, 'Insanity, Illinois.' " He nodded and scribbled on the papers. "That'll hunt. Are you still planning on giving Terry half the byline credit? This story is all over the tube, and we've got the exclusive inside story."

"Terry earned it," I said.

I escaped the office without further questioning and found Jimmy waiting for me on the sidewalk outside. "Hi," he said with a smile. "You ready to go?"

I nodded. "What have you got planned?"

He eyed the food in my hands. "I was going to suggest we go out to lunch," he said. "But it looks like you've already eaten."

"Don't change your plans on my account. Lunch sounds great." I shoved the last of the burger into my mouth and swallowed it quickly. "But don't think you're going to get off that easy."

"What do you mean?"

I stepped up to him and tapped a finger against his chest. "I mean I expect dinner, too. Maybe a movie, I haven't decided yet."

Jimmy laughed. "Aren't you tired?"

"Exhausted," I replied. "But this time you're not getting away. This is going to be a real date."

"A real date," Jimmy repeated. He hooked his arm through mine and steered me down the sidewalk. "All right. I guess it's time we tried it."

I leaned against his shoulder. "That's what I've been saying all along."

LAURELL K. HAMILTON _

"Hamilton takes her world by the teeth and runs with it."—_Locus_

It's hunting season! _And the most feared vampire hunter returns..._

__THE KILLING DANCE__   0-441-00452-0/$6.50

With a price on her head and professional killers on her trail, Anita Blake, preternatural expert and vampire killer extraordinaire, turns to the men in her life for help. Which in her case, means an alpha werewolf and a master vampire.

She needs as much protection as possible, human or otherwise. But Anita's beginning to wonder if two monsters are better than one...

BLOODY BONES	0-441-00374-5/$6.50
THE LUNATIC CAFE	0-441-00293-5/$6.50
CIRCUS OF THE DAMNED	0-441-00197-1/$6.50
THE LAUGHING CORPSE	0-441-00091-6/$6.50
GUILTY PLEASURES	0-441-30483-4/$6.50

"You'll want to read it in one sitting—I did."—P. N. Elrod

Payable in U.S. funds. No cash accepted. Postage & handling: $1.75 for one book, 75¢ for each additional. Maximum postage $5.50. Prices, postage and handling charges may change without notice. Visa, Amex, MasterCard call 1-800-788-6262, ext. 1, or fax 1-201-933-2316; refer to ad #723

Or, check above books   Bill my: ☐ Visa ☐ MasterCard ☐ Amex _____ (expires)
and send this order form to:
The Berkley Publishing Group   Card#_____

P.O. Box 12289, Dept. B   Daytime Phone #_____ ($10 minimum)

Newark, NJ 07101-5289   Signature_____

Please allow 4-6 weeks for delivery.   Or enclosed is my: ☐ check ☐ money order
Foreign and Canadian delivery 8-12 weeks.

Ship to:

Name_____   Book Total $_____

Address_____   Applicable Sales Tax $_____
     (NY, NJ, PA, CA, GST Can.)

City_____   Postage & Handling $_____

State/ZIP_____   Total Amount Due $_____

Bill to: Name_____

Address_____   City_____

State/ZIP_____

P. N. ELROD

"Offers deft touches of wit, beauty, and suspense.
Entertaining."   —*Publishers Weekly*

__DANCE OF DEATH   0-441-00309-5/$5.99
In P. N. Elrod's latest novel, the vampire Jonathan
Barrett meets the mortal son he never knew he had.

__DEATH AND THE MAIDEN   0-441-00071-1/$4.99

__RED DEATH   0-441-71094-8/$4.99

THE VAMPIRE FILES

"An entertaining blend of detective story and the supernatural
from a promising new writer." —*Science Fiction Chronicle*

__BLOODCIRCLE   0-441-06717-4/$4.99

__FIRE IN THE BLOOD   0-441-85946-1/$4.50

Payable in U.S. funds. No cash accepted. Postage & handling: $1.75 for one book, 75¢ for each additional.
Maximum postage $5.50. Prices, postage and handling charges may change without notice. Visa,
Amex, MasterCard call 1-800-788-6262, ext. 1, or fax 1-201-933-2316; refer to ad # 535a

Or, check above books   Bill my: ☐ Visa ☐ MasterCard ☐ Amex _____ (expires)
and send this order form to:
The Berkley Publishing Group   Card# _____
P.O. Box 12289, Dept. B   ($10 minimum)
Newark, NJ 07101-5289   Daytime Phone # _____
                             Signature _____
Please allow 4-6 weeks for delivery.   Or enclosed is my: ☐ check ☐ money order
Foreign and Canadian delivery 8-12 weeks.
Ship to:
Name_____   Book Total $_____
Address_____   Applicable Sales Tax $_____
                                          (NY, NJ, PA, CA, GST Can.)
City_____   Postage & Handling $_____
State/ZIP_____   Total Amount Due $_____
Bill to: Name_____
Address_____City_____
State/ZIP_____

"If The Cat Who...*books could meet 'The X-Files,'*
the adventures of Savvy McKinnon would be the
result."—Laurell K. Hamilton

NEWS FROM THE EDGE

by Mark Sumner

The Monster of Minnesota   0-441-00459-8/$5.99

"BIG JELLY" FILLS BELLY WITH FOUR NEW VICTIMS!
Sure, thinks Savannah "Savvy" McKinnon, maybe those people
were killed by the lake monster known as Big Jelly. But maybe
not. If there's a cover-up to be exposed, she's just the one to do it.

Insanity, Illinois   0-441-00511-X/$5.99

It's a normal day at the *Global Query*—calls, calls, calls—from a
housewife menaced by her appliances...a farmer with a volcano
in his apple orchard...a man with snow geese in his toilet...and of
course, a guy talking to God through his TV. Typical.

Until Savvy realizes that all the calls came from the same town
in Illinois...

VISIT PUTNAM BERKLEY ONLINE ON THE INTERNET:
http://www.berkley.com

Payable in U.S. funds. No cash accepted. Postage & handling: $1.75 for one book, 75¢ for each
additional. Maximum postage $5.50. Prices, postage and handling charges may change without
notice. Visa, Amex, MasterCard call 1-800-788-6262, ext. 1, or fax 1-201-933-2316; refer to ad #771

Or, check above books   Bill my: ☐ Visa ☐ MasterCard ☐ Amex _____ (expires)
and send this order form to:
The Berkley Publishing Group   Card#_____
P.O. Box 12289, Dept. B   **($10 minimum)**
Newark, NJ 07101-5289   Daytime Phone #_____
                          Signature_____
Please allow 4-6 weeks for delivery.   Or enclosed is my: ☐ check ☐ money order
Foreign and Canadian delivery 8-12 weeks.
Ship to:
Name_____   Book Total $_____
Address_____   Applicable Sales Tax $_____
                                          (NY, NJ, PA, CA, GST Can.)
City_____   Postage & Handling $_____
State/ZIP_____   Total Amount Due $_____
Bill to: Name_____
Address_____   City_____
State/ZIP_____

PUTNAM *pb* BERKLEY

online

Your Internet gateway to a virtual
environment with hundreds of
entertaining and enlightening books
from the Putnam Berkley Group.

While you're there visit the PB Café and
order-up the latest buzz on the best
authors and books around—Tom Clancy,
Patricia Cornwell, W.E.B. Griffin,
Nora Roberts, William Gibson,
Robin Cook, Brian Jacques, Jan Brett,
Catherine Coulter and many more!

Putnam Berkley Online is located at
http://www.putnam.com

• •

PB PLUG

Once a month we serve up the dish on the
latest science fiction, fantasy, and horror
titles currently on sale. Plus you'll get
interviews of your favorite authors, trivia,
a top ten list, and so much more
fun it's shameless.

Check out PB Plug at http://www.pbplug.com
• •